The
Broken
Bow

PATH OF PROMISE

THE BROKEN BOW

Lithia tells two lies to protect her son. Time is running out. Tomorrow they are doomed to die. . . .

LaJoyce Martin

The Broken Bow

by LaJoyce Martin

©1996, Word Aflame Press
Hazelwood, MO 63042-2299

Cover design by Paul Povolni
Cover art by Glenn Myers

All Scripture quotations in this book are from the King James Version of the Bible unless otherwise identified.

Printed in United States of America

Printed by

Library of Congress Cataloging-in-Publication Data

Martin, LaJoyce, 1937–
    The broken bow / by LaJoyce Martin.
        p.   cm.
   ISBN 1-56722-139-4 (pbk.)
   1. Indians of North America—West (U.S.)—Fiction. 2. Mothers and sons—West (U.S.)—Fiction. 3. Frontier and pioneer life—West (U.S.)—Fiction. I. Title.
PS3563.A72486B76   1996
813'.54—dc20
                                    96-11682
                                        CIP

Contents

Chapter One

The Brave

Moccasin-shod feet were running, then they slowed and stopped at the door of her pueblo.

"Lithia! They're coming!"

With much effort, Lithia raised her bulky form from the elk-skin cot. "Who?" Her mind grappled for relief from her anxiety but found only fear.

"The braves. They're bringing your Victor. He's wounded."

She should be glad for the disclosure, she told herself, and she was, albeit she bitterly resented the bearer of the tidings. Keeta, the tribe's self-appointed newsmonger, made it her business to know everything about everybody at all times. Then she let her findings slide from her tongue, revised to her own proclivity.

"Is he injured badly?"

"I don't know, but I'll find out."

"No, never mind, Keeta—"

The feet were running again, their zealous thud dying away like a distant and retreating drum.

Lithia readied Victor's bed with an appalling foreboding. *At least he is alive,* she told herself, shutting a mental door against the chill of panic that crept up from some chamber of her being—a room where pictures of horrors were kept. *Whatever the damage, I'll nurse him back to health. I can't lose him with the birth of our child so near.*

Her chin went up. After all, didn't her name mean "a stone"? Even with the disadvantage of her condition, she would be strong and gritty. She took a deep breath in an attempt to calm herself.

The wait was not a long one. She beat down anger with inner fists when she heard the same busy feet approaching again. Keeta knew before she did. . . .

"He's hurt dreadfully, Lithia."

The four warriors came slowly, packing Victor on a makeshift stretcher. The slightest movement brought a moan from his lips. As they lowered him to his bunk, none would meet Lithia's questioning eyes. Little was said, but much was understood.

"We will come anytime you call for us," one of them spoke up. The meaning was implied and clear: *We will come for his body.* "Send Keeta." Thus saying, they stole from the pueblo and were gone.

They thought he would die, and they thought it would be best. But he wouldn't. Lithia squatted beside her husband and caressed his face, running her fingers gently through his hair, slippery with sweat. "You will be whole again, my valiant one," she crooned. "I will see to it."

He looked up at her through pain-glazed eyes. "I shall die, Lithia," he said without preamble. "The medicine iron from the white man's fire machine is inside my body. The white enemy hurled the thunderbolt and . . . and it struck me in the middle—" he winced.

"No, you shall *not* die! I will not allow it!" Had she

8

spoken the words, or had they thundered in her veins? "And why the chieftain does not let the white man be is more than I can comprehend! Why did he attack the colony, anyhow?"

"You do not understand, my Lithia." Victor talked to her in a patient, placating tone. "The white men gobble up the countryside, destroying the timber and ravaging the wildlife. They cover the earth like a plague of grasshoppers. They put up fences and set fires to the grasses and claim the mountains for their own. Soon there will be no buffalo, no forests, and no land left for our sons and their sons.

"How can a man own land? It is like the air, given to us to use as we need it. People who take more than they need are like the bee who stores honey; it will be taken from them.

"The white man presses us to sign treaties. They would whittle us away until there is nothing left but shavings to be trampled underfoot. They would drive us to extinction in the dust of insult. But we will never put our names to anything that takes our rivers or our pathless woods! We cannot trust the white man; he changes the words after the signing.

"If we do not run the enemy away, we will lose our valleys, our homes, our mountains and go toward the setting sun to worthless land the white man doesn't want. We will be always moving.

"The white man lusts for land and money. He sees our trees as nothing but lumber. He has not learned that the woods will feed him if he lives *with* them instead of exploiting them. Our tribesmen would never cut down a living tree, for a tree is the life of the forest.

"The white man steals our heritage. We do not wish our history and rhythm disturbed, but until he has despoiled and murdered and violated our way of life, he is unappeased. That is why we fight. We are trying to preserve our future."

No longer than the explanation was, it took much of his strength, and his spirit seemed to slip farther back in his eyes.

Lithia said no more. She moved heavily about the room, preparing strong broth for him with a mien of determination. "These lobelia leaves will help you to breathe easier," she said.

"You are wasting your while, my sweet doe," he met her eyes only for a flicker or two. "Time has set its face against me."

"What you say is all wind and no weather," she refuted, trying hard to discipline the emotion out of her voice. Then she laid the side of her forehead against his cheek. "You will live for me . . . and for your unborn son."

Lithia spent a wakeful night in spite of her weariness. Deserted by sleep, she tossed and thrashed. A hatchet of sentiment chopped her mind into pieces: the past, the present, and the future. Her parents were gone, and she had no brother or sister. Victor was her life. What would she do if she lost him? In the darkness, her heart felt hammered and sore—and she was afraid.

At last, a blade of gray morning sliced the sky, and there was enough light for her to see her husband's face. An expression of pain punctured the thin wall of his uneasy sleep: his lips were stretched taut against his teeth. But he had made it through the night!

Birds, awakening, made fusses and twitters while the morning breeze set up a low whistle in the trees. Then the gray light eased the shadows away, and Lithia felt better in the gold of dawn. She peeled the sweet root and put it on to boil.

That's when she heard the running feet again. Keeta

was out early, garnering green and fermenting information. She must not be allowed to disturb Victor.

Lithia stepped outside. A freshening wind touched her face, relieving the sting in her eyes from lack of sleep.

"I came to ask about Victor." Keeta's manner teetered on the edge of rudeness.

"Victor is doing well, thank you. He had a good night and he is resting."

"I heard the screech of an owl making his mournful call. The grandmothers say the cry of an owl means someone will die, and I wondered . . ." Keeta had arrow-shaped eyes and the ability to pierce with them.

Lithia sheltered her thoughts behind long eyelashes. It seemed nature intended that she and Keeta be antagonists. "He is sleeping. Sleep is healing."

"The warriors said—"

"Excuse me, Keeta. I hear Victor stirring, so I must give him his tea." Her voice gathered strength until she sounded calm and confident, not at all like the frightened woman she was. She took a step backward. "But I think he isn't up to having visitors just yet." The gesture managed to convey dismissal.

A seep of blackened blood oozed from Victor's side, and Lithia cleansed the wound religiously. "It looks better," she told him on the third day. "The skin is healing."

"Only the surface heals," he replied. "The thunderbolt is working on the inside. I can feel it. It gnaws like the chewing of a rodent. My skin is hot and my belly is bloated. It is but a matter of time, and I shall lie in Mother Earth's bosom. But I go honorably. You must rear our son to be brave and fearless. Death is no disgrace if it is faced with courage. Give my son my name, and I shall live on through him." Victor closed his eyes. An acre of

11

silence lay between them. They were already parting to unconnected worlds.

"Victor! Oh, my Victor!" A cry of rage burst from Lithia. "I have not seen twenty summers! You cannot leave a squaw so young! And—and with child!" The words tumbled out before she could modify them.

Surely if she prayed to the gods passionately enough, she told herself, she could hold him in life. If her prayers wearied, she would be letting him slip down into death. She must pray and pray, daring not sleep lest she lose her hold. But when his eyes sank deeper into the shadows, a spasm of distress twisted her mouth; nameless wails filled her soul.

"Shall I call for the witch doctor, Victor?" She moved toward the door to follow her words. "I thought that my prayers and cures would make you well, but surely the doctor can do something. I'll go for him now."

"No, Lithia." His voice was but a whisper, as empty as a wasp nest in winter, his spirit and will gone. "You are afraid of the witch doctor, and I would not want to put you in jeopardy of an untimely birth."

"I shall make my fears turn their heads away! I shall make them look toward the wall while the witch doctor is here. Please let me fetch him!"

"No." He wrapped his weak words in finality. "I do not want the witch doctor. Behind his wretched masks, he is nothing but a powerless man like myself. He can do nothing to stay death or to prolong life. The bitter medicines and cruel pummelings I cannot abide. Let me go peacefully. I want only your gentle hands until . . . the end." His expression became vacant, and he spoke no more. The coma that took him mercifully swept away all his pain; his shallow, listless breathing barely disturbed the contour of his ribs.

Victor lived for two more days. Lithia entertained the

same hopes at sunrise—and the same despair at eve. For hours, she sat beside him and watched, willing his chest to rise and fall, fighting back nausea. It seemed that every breath he took might be his last, but it went on and on and on. Her world whirled round and round, spinning itself into a dark, narrowing funnel.

On his last evening, the twilight lingered, a soft blue glow. The top of the tallest tree caught the dying ray of sun from the west, then the bough turned slowly to black.

The tiny spark of life in Victor went out during the night. Until that moment, Lithia had hoped even though the hope had been forlorn. Now it was gone as in the silence she looked at silence.

Victor was dead. It was so absolute it closed over her like a shroud. He would never come home from a hunt again; he would never hold her in his arms again. The love that brightened her life like a second sun was gone from the world. Alone, she was cut in two. If only she could go with him. . . .

A terrible, choking lump that began in her throat broke into tearless sobs. Entombed in grief, she sent for the men who had brought him to come and remove his body for burial.

Chapter Two

The Ritual

"I have come to stay with you until the burying of your brave on the morrow," Keeta said, bringing with her a wondering, curious tension. "You could birth suddenly with the shock you've had. A death and a birth on the same day are a bad omen."

"I'll be all right, Keeta. You may go." Lithia felt sick and weak, her self-control impossibly stretched. She wanted to be alone; she needed to make mental sandbags to keep back the waters while she built her wall for the future.

"Oh, no! I must stay with you and see how you fare tonight, Lithia. Then I will be able to tell the tribe whether or not you held your name without flinching. How could I know if you cheated with tears if I were not here?"

Lithia focused her burning eyes on Keeta. She weighed her words with care; every one seemed a hundred pounds. "I have learned that I am no stone, Keeta. My heart can be broken as easily as a bird's egg. I have lost everything: my mother, my father, and now my husband. I have a right to tears."

"Life is full of losses, Lithia. Hopes sink with the old day and rise with the new. We'll see if the star that is a hunter with a pack on his back comes out in the northwest tonight. If it does, that means you will marry again."

No amount of wishing could send Keeta away. She hovered about Lithia's pueblo, babbling with tiresome endlessness. She looked into every gourd bowl and under every blanket. Her voice rasped on, trespassing on Lithia's nerves. "It is aloneness that makes death so terrible, but soon you will have a child and your sorrows will vanish in a gust of joy. My son, Slate, fills every corner of my heart. . . ." She yammered on until Lithia was too distressed to hear more.

Lithia's bed, with its springy softness of elk-hide webbing stretched on a frame of hickory posts, helped to absorb her profound grief. Victor had made the bed for her when they were married. She would never forget the day they each held an end of the marriage stick and smiled into the other's eyes. Victor claimed she had the priceless ability to put the zest of life into others, but she thought it was the other way around. *He* brought joy to *her*. Would time ever blunt the spike of memory?

Keeta disrupted the pleasant daydream. "Are you asleep so soon, Lithia? One would suppose a widow would not sleep while her husband's body is being prepared for burial!"

Lithia pretended sleep to escape Keeta's monotonous prattle, and as soon as darkness gave her a covering, she pulled Victor's doeskin shirt from behind the bed and hugged it to herself. The garment still carried his masculine scent; it was her only solace and sole luxury while the bewilderment and frustration passed through her body.

"Lithia!" The coarse whisper sounded too loud. "I think that star is out. Lucky you! You're sure to remarry . . ."

Lithia stopped her ears with Victor's shirt.

Night went by and dawn colors flamed in the sky, full and beautiful. The morning's serenity was ironic, an antonym to everything Lithia felt. It seemed to mock her consummate hollowness.

Jibbering and shallow, Keeta urged her to get dressed and led her to the burial site. A large crowd had gathered, ranked in accordance to custom: older men in front, young men behind them, squaws and children on the outskirts. It seemed the whole tribe was there and that they were all watching her. Each step cost her an effort.

The chief of the Kotopaxi tribe officiated at the ceremony. The proceedings began decorously with the raising of the chieftain's hand. "Today will be a time for rejoicing," he said. "In this mighty tribe, bravery is the surest way to honor. And the gods pay honor to the bravest of all braves this day."

As he talked on, Lithia learned what her husband did not tell her: when the white man shot at the tribe's leader, Victor flung himself between the chief and his enemy "with a speed like lightning." It was Victor's body that took the death blow meant for another while the tribal warriors filled the air with exultant shouts that their chief had been saved. There had been much dancing and jubilation.

Lithia experienced a moment of swelling pride. They were talking about *her* Victor. No arm was stronger than his, no heart more fearless. The consolation she felt, however, was short-lived. She hid her face when the witch doctor put in his appearance with hideous motions and a frightening mask.

Keeta punched Lithia with her elbow. "No, Lithia! Don't cover your face. It is not proper. The witch doctor will think you are ungrateful."

"Ungrateful?"

"Yes. You must be grateful that it was your husband and not our chief who lost his life!" She spoke in a hissed whisper.

The witch doctor was talking. "Chief and tribesmen of the mighty Kotopaxi tribe: I have invited the gods to the obsequies of Brave Victor. They will join us as we rejoice this day." His oration incited the people. They were enraptured.

The witch doctor then proceeded to carry on a one-sided conversation with the spirits to impress his listeners. Some claimed there was fire in his words; surely, they said, he communicated with the Other Land.

According to the doctor, the gods were walking Victor all the way to his next world destination because he had saved the chief. To have their escort was the highest of favors. He gave a point by point update on the trek. "Now they are striding along beside a stream that bubbles down rock-bound, fern-fringed stairs," he said. "He is halfway between two worlds." He made a dramatic pause. "Now a great light has burst over them like fire from the sky, showering them with glitter."

These things Lithia only dimly understood, only half heard, because Victor was gone and nothing else mattered.

The witch doctor stopped again and shook a rattle for emphasis. "And now the wind is singing with them as they thread their way through the woods to journey's end . . ."

Journey's end. Lithia's gloom bit with renewed torture. *Journey's end.* What did it mean? Where was her Victor? He had left her, and she had an urge to leap into the grave and go with him to—wherever.

If the medium's liturgy was meant to console her, it didn't. Victor didn't want the witch doctor beside him when he was dying, and she was certain he wouldn't wish his cortege now. The old man had a way of showing up at all special occasions, happy or sad. And where he was, he took over. Lithia turned her mind off, too weary, too utterly dejected to listen any longer.

Robed in the chieftain's own blanket, Victor's body was painted red for bravery. Lithia would have preferred that they leave Victor's skin its natural color of polished walnut. But they didn't ask her.

The same four warriors who brought Victor to her when he was injured took him to his grave. They dropped in his bow, his quiver, and his quartz-tipped arrow feathered with red hawk tail. Three lines on a wooden headstone denoted victories of his short lifetime. The chief commended Lithia for having such a courageous husband, a noble member whose sacrifice paid credit to both himself and the Kotopaxi tribe.

"Oooo! Lithia, the chief looks your way!" Keeta gave her an envious jab. "To gain the chief's attention is the secret lust of every woman. Why, I'd be *dizzy* with excitement!"

Lithia showed only indifference. She would gladly have traded the glory of a thousand tribal chiefs with their implacable pomposity for one more moment with her beloved Victor.

Why should the life of a chief be of more value than the life of her own loved one? The chief had no wife and Victor did. Victor's wife and unborn child needed him. Was she expected to be *happy* that her husband was dead and the chief yet alive? It seemed so. A contradictory jumble of emotions filled her breast, and she was lost in a miasma of helpless anger.

After the funeral, the tribesmen streamed back

toward the tribal camp. They started singing, softly at first and then louder and somehow jovial. By the time they reached the village, they were openly boasting, riotous and shouting.

With her heart encased in pain, Lithia hurried from the cemetery, pueblo eager. Unable to express her grief openly, she sought the solitude of her home—and Victor's—to hide away with her heartache and loneliness. She wanted no witnesses to her weakness, to her whimpering agony.

She worried that Keeta would intrude, but Keeta's son became ill, confining her to her own quarters. No one came with condolences, and Lithia was glad. She dragged through the hours, waking to misery—walking with it, lying down with it. The days crumbled away as if chiseled from the calendar, nameless and wrenched from their purpose.

Tranquilizers come in many forms, and Lithia found hers in the bittersweet memories of the fleeting days she and Victor shared. When she thought of him, his face came before her so close and endearing that she could not see around it.

They'd had good days. Their marriage, she told herself, had the flavor of a life worth tasting. Victor had mantled her with care and cosseting. He was forever bringing her gifts, sweet, foolish gifts: colorful beetles and butterflies, resin to chew, odd-shaped rocks. He had been proud of his bride's artistry—and she'd sunned herself in his open adulation. She had decorated the walls of their adobe home with the animal designs and geometric figures that he liked best. . . .

Remembering brought pleasure, but it brought pain, too. Victor did not live to see the son he had set his heart upon. He'd been so excited at her announcement that he'd gone out and trapped a white rabbit to make the baby's first breechcloth. And he'd built a hardwood cradle. Now Lithia would have to face the birth of her child without him. She tightened her mind against the thought.

As the days passed over her, she learned that it was easier to perform known duties than to prowl wistfully among memories. Victor had once told her that one must neither long for tomorrow nor waste regret on yesterday.

Ah, but it was hard. . . .

Chapter Three

The Broken Bow

"You must work a little harder, Lithia. How soon the end will come depends on you." Mamu, the tribal midwife, sat on the floor, waiting for the advent of birth. She had been summoned before daylight.

No one knew how old Mamu was; no one could remember so far back. Her genesis was lost in the mists of legend. She had attended Lithia's mother when Lithia was born and Lithia's grandmother when Lithia's mother was born. Some of the clansmen vowed that she was timeless; she'd always been and would always be.

Lithia thought Mamu was showing signs of advanced age, though. Her shriveled skin clung to her bones as if she'd been smoked in an oven; it was wilted and dried like jerky. Her teeth had fallen out, and her hearing was poor. But her eyesight still served her well.

"I'm tired, Mamu," complained Lithia.

"Eh?"

"I'm tired."

"Shoo. Shoo. Victor would shame you. Your pain

23

does not compare with his, and he didn't whimper. His spirit is watching now, expecting you to bring his son into the world without grousing."

"Yes, Mamu."

"And you had best hurry. Here comes the morning sun. Early morning babies are the healthiest."

"I'm hurrying, Mamu."

"You're taking time to fret."

"I'm sorry."

"And what will you name this fine son?"

"He will be named Victor for his father. That was his father's last request."

"Shoo. Shoo. And we hope that he will be as fine a specimen of manhood."

Lithia smiled slightly, a mere twist of the lips. "Yes, Mamu. But what if he is a girl child?"

"Not a chance," said she. "I can tell before a child is born what he will be, and I've never missed. It is the gift of wisdom."

"I . . . I wish Victor was here." Lithia wrestled with a raw loneliness. Where did the physical pain end and the emotional pain begin?

"Shoo. Shoo. There you go whining again," scolded the midwife. "Wishing is a waste of time. Think only of the unendurable joy you will know when you hold your son to your bosom. You cannot relax now."

Pangs of fatigue throbbed in every fiber of Lithia's body, sweeping over her like an avalanche, almost driving consciousness away. Her breath sawed in and out through dry lips.

"The more one endures, the better one is able to endure."

"I'm . . . t-trying . . ."

"Shoo. Shoo. You are dallying. I am ashamed of you."

Suddenly, Lithia stiffened in a throe of travail and it

was over. Mamu held a squirming infant in her brittle, old hands. With an effort, she withdrew her eyes from him. "It's a boy all right," she said. She gave Lithia an odd, calculating look. "But—"

"But *what?*"

Mamu's silence only served to increase the awful uncertainty that hung, unvoiced, in the room. Time held its breath in suspense.

"He's cursed."

"Cursed?" Runaway thoughts shattered Lithia's short-term happiness. *"Cursed?"* she repeated.

"Yes. He is a broken bow." Mamu's voice was flat, emotionless. "He is not worthy of his brave father's name. You must call him Broken Bow."

Broken Bow. Lithia shrank from the name; she loathed it. It would forever brand her son. Anything but this. . . . *"Where* is he broken?" There was pleading in Lithia's voice. Her dreams for her child melted, leaving a puddle of reality colder than snow broth. "Oh, Mamu! Say it is not so!"

"His right hand is missing. It is a whim of the gods. He must die."

"No! No!" Lithia screamed it. "He is my hope for the future! I cannot bear it!" Despair cramped her stomach as she cried out in protest against this added cruelty of fate. Wasn't it enough that she had lost Victor? Must she lose her baby, too?

Summoning all her strength, she snatched the infant from the frail midwife and held him close. Fury surged within her. *He will not die!* But wait . . . hadn't she said these words before?

"Shoo. Shoo. It is a pity, Lithia. Back, back into the yesterdays the gods have delved to uncover a fault. They are merciless, these gods. I would that it had not happened to you."

Lithia's life passed before her in an instant. What had she ever done to deserve this punishment? Or was it her husband's deed? Or her mother's? Or her grandmother's? Why had the vengeful gods struck out at her? *She* had never defied them.

How these unforgiving spirits held grudges! They had a way of settling a score after many years. Some far removed ancestor had displeased them. Mamu said it was possible that the hand of a great-great-grandfather had carelessly hurled a stone at a god and struck it. The gods could forebear no longer; the debt must be paid. Lithia was chosen to atone for the sin.

A floodgate of contempt was opened, letting her reservoir of respect for her forerunners wash away. Why did these heedless relatives leave their guilt for her innocent baby to bear? They were adults, hardy and strong. Why could they not take the responsibility for their own foolish debts? And the gods—they could have as easily repaid Victor's *bravery* by sending her a robust, healthy baby! But no, they always found a negative act to carp about.

As she held her small papoose, the target of an old and disgruntled enemy, a tear dropped onto his head—a head scarcely larger than Mamu's gourd of medicines. They were helpless, she and this baby, in the whirlwind of revenge.

What kind of god would vent his wrath on a creature so fragile? Who could worship any image or spirit who would be as cruel as this? There was no righteousness in it! Lithia knew these were iniquitous thoughts and forbidden, but she did not care.

"I must report the curse to the chieftain," Mamu was saying. "You well know his rule, Lithia. He weeds out the weak and spares only the strong. And he will make no exception for your son—"

"It is a senseless rule!" Anger pinched off Lithia's breath as her sense of outrage grew. "What chieftain in his right mind could become rooted in the wicked conviction that attaining one's end lies in slaughtering the innocent?"

"All your protests will avail nothing, Lithia. It is the custom of the centuries. And if you try to hide your child, you will only delay the inevitable. It will be easier to part with him now than later when your heart is matted to him."

"But surely the chieftain will remember that Victor saved his life but a moon ago! Would not such a deed be sufficient grounds to spare my baby's life?" Lithia, her eyes smoldering, flung the words at Mamu. Her throat was thick and full.

"Hold your mouth and listen to me, Lithia. Have you gone mad? The chieftain cannot break the age-old rule of banishing the inadequate for you or anyone else. That would surely dilute his strength in warfare. Soon we would become an inferior race. The chief must have only the best in his tribe. Anything less must go. Life does not make allowances for mistakes. Who would think of going to war with a broken bow, a blunt arrow, or a lame horse? Shoo. Shoo. A broken bow—that's what your son is."

"But if he were the chief's own son—" argued Lithia.

"It would make no difference. The chief is impartial. His own father was killed when he became incapacitated. The chieftain was a witness to the death and never quailed."

A fine bead of sweat formed on Lithia's upper lip. Was there any way to save her child?

"To be stronger than one's foes and to win favor with the gods are the two most important goals in life. And for these two goals the chief lives, regardless of the consequences or pain it might cause himself or others."

"I will go before the chief and plead for the life of my son on Victor's behalf."

"Shoo. Shoo. Many words will only infuriate him. He is a proud man. You dare not make him angry."

Lithia's heart sank. She felt ground down like acorns beneath the pestle, overwhelmed with the agony of her predicament. "You will tell him . . . today?"

"He is gone. I will tell him when he returns from the autumn hunt. I am not happy to do this, but it is my duty. Goodbye, Lithia." With the look and pace of an ancient tortoise, Mamu gathered her herbs and left the pueblo.

Lithia pulled her child to her breast as the day dozed away to its end. At least he wouldn't be killed on the day of his birth. She would have him for a few hours and he would feel her love. He wouldn't go to his tiny grave without knowing a mother's care. She brooded through the sleepless night, stingy with each moment she yet had to nurture Victor's son.

The annual hunt provided food for the tribe during the winter months. The chieftain was particular about when they hunted; Victor had told Lithia this. "If you hunt the animals while they are trying to raise their young, there will be none eventually," he had said. "If we work with nature, nature will work with us."

Sometimes the hunters were gone for a week and sometimes for a month or more, depending on the location and plenitude of the game. The witch doctor (Lithia shuddered) directed the hunters to an area suggested by the gods. Lithia hoped that the spiritualist had sent them on a long trip this year; that would give her more time to gain strength and prepare herself for the parting that lay ahead.

In spite of the witch doctor's blessings, the hunters didn't always find food. If the catch was small this fall, the chieftain would be choleric. But if the hunt went well, he might celebrate with a feast before his audience with Mamu.

Lithia's mind put as many days—and as many obstacles—as possible between her and the moment of truth. With every sun that rose, her affection for the child added a new dimension. How she loved him! None of the dreadful curses conjured up by the gods could dampen her fondness for the papoose. His smiles and gurgles dissipated her sadness, vanquishing her fog of wretchedness like ruptured cobwebs. This child needed her and she needed him—and the love they shared was bigger than both of them. Why, she would give her life for him!

No one would take her baby from her; she would find a way to save him. She gave way to wishful thinking, closing a trap door deep in her mind. At times it seemed she must sit on that awful door, using all her weight to keep it shut, and in spite of all her strength, it would open a crack ere she could bolt it down again. . . .

Two moons passed before the triumphant sounds of successful hunters filled the evening air. By this time, Lithia's heart was knit to her Broken Bow with needles of motherly passion. No one could resist such an adorable child. *If the chieftain sees him, he cannot kill him.*

Even now, she was making preparations for the chieftains' unavoidable call.

Chapter Four

Reprieve

The feast of hunters lasted for seven days with all other tribal business suspended for the duration. Dancing, laughter, and exchanging of gifts laid bare emotions unmatched at any other tribal festivity; even the stoics screamed and shouted with wild abandon.

The chieftain's jocular mood was contagious, spurring the tribe to sportive celebration. Roast bison, parched corn and pemmican—venison into which fresh berries had been pounded—kept the tribesmen filled and milling about until the late hours of the night.

Victor had taken part in the celebration last year, and Lithia knew the order of events by rote. To highlight the festival, the oldest of the hunters pointed the stem of his pipe in six directions: north, south, east, west, up and down. When Lithia asked Victor the reason for the strange rite, he'd said it was a necessary part of the jubilee, its meaning never questioned. That was the difference between Lithia and Victor. She always questioned; he accepted without question.

Each family was allotted a share of the food. Lithia's mouth watered thinking of the fresh meat, but she stayed in her pueblo, heart heavy. If she ate tonight, the food would only stick in her throat. The partying would cease soon and Mamu would give her report. Lithia's short journey with hope had left her abandoned on the shores of realism—and the tide was coming in.

She followed the proceedings with her ears. When the frenzied stamping, leaping, and beating of drums began, she knew that the hunter who had bagged the trophy buffalo was being honored. One year it had been her own Victor. That was before they were wed, but she had been proud of him. She thought that might have been the evening her heart was smitten with great admiration for him.

Next came the boasting contest. She suspected that few of the stories were ungarnished, but exaggeration seemed to be the name of the game. Every hunter shouted his deeds, making an ear-splitting racket. This had always been a favorite part of the celebration for Lithia, and as it began, she moved closer to the door in hopes of catching snatches of their tales. She was tempted to step outside where the blur of smoke smudged the orange of the evening sky, but she dare not take Broken Bow into public view. There would be other feasts, but never another firstborn. . . . She sliced the thought in half.

The direction of the wind was right for her to hear some of the embroidery. The king of hunters told how he wore a mask to stalk his prize. "I chanted over the mask so that it would have power to attract the animals," he yelled. He went into florid detail, most of which Lithia missed.

Another hunter described holding a leaf to his lips, simulating the cry of a fawn to woo a magnificent doe to himself. The doe, thinking her offspring in distress, answered his call. Something in the story made Lithia shiver as if she were cold; Victor had called her his little doe. . . .

Still another braggart said he prayed to the birds for assistance. To show his appreciation for their help, he killed the animal and offered the liver and heart to the birds as a reward. Apprehension formed a lump in Lithia's loins; she wanted to listen, yet she didn't want to hear. Every story struck a tender soreness inside of her.

"It is because we have not compromised that the gods have smiled upon us!" the chief's voice thundered. "It is because we will have no weaklings! The Kotopaxi tribe is the strongest and best in the world. And we will keep it that way." A roar of applause went up from the hunters. "Long live the Kotopaxis! Long live the gods of the Kotopaxis!"

Soul-shaken, Lithia sprang back from the door, her courage diminishing each moment. Why had she ever hoped that the chieftain might change his mind? She put her hand over her heart as if she had taken a mortal blow; she felt that she might faint. The chief had reaffirmed his stand in a voice firm and final.

The feasting began, the air laden with the pungent smells of smoked meat and parched corn. But nothing, however aromatic, could awaken Lithia's appetite. It mattered not if she ever ate again. If her baby must die, why would she wish to remain alive?

Then Lithia heard the running feet. They slowed and stopped at her door.

"Why are you not at the festival, Lithia?" Keeta poked her head in at the front opening.

"I am sick." Lithia feigned a headache. "But the churning in my belly has passed and I shall soon be well," she added quickly, lest Keeta should send the witch doctor with medicines. "I'm yet weak from the birthing." The milk-and-water smile she tried on fit poorly; she hoped it was convincing enough.

Keeta's eyes riveted to the sleeping baby. Only his head was visible. While most infants remained unclothed in warm weather, Lithia had wrapped her son in a blanket to hide his small arm with the missing hand.

"It is autumn, Lithia—and hot," scolded Keeta. "Do you know nothing about caring for babies? Unwrap the child so that his body will be cool. Why, your pueblo is like an oven!" She started to remove the blanket, but Lithia grabbed her hand vehemently.

"I will wait until he awakens, Keeta," she said, her heart pounding from the close call. "He sleeps more securely swaddled." With much effort, Lithia managed to keep her temper wrapped, too. "According to Mamu, each baby is different."

"You have not been out in the village to show your son," pointed out the busybody. "I had planned to visit you on the day of your son's birth, but Slate was ill. In fact, I would have been with you when you birthed if I had not been confined with my own son's fever."

"A child is not a thing for display, Keeta. Neither is a birthing. I have my own reasons for not exposing my son to anything that might harm him at such a young age—"

"Too protective you are, Lithia. Indeed, what could harm him? Of course, most of the clan will overlook your foolish indulgence since you so recently lost Victor."

"I . . . I hope so." Keeta could learn little from what was left unsaid.

"And what did you name your long-awaited son?"

Lithia hesitated—and Keeta waited with sharp, weasel attention, her arrow-shaped eyes flinty.

"Victor asked me to give him his name, but I call him my Little Bow." She didn't look up.

"Little Bow," repeated Keeta with a touch of mockery. "Such sentimentality is silly to me, but to each her own. *I'd* call him Victor and let him grow up to be a *man* instead of a mollycoddled, squaw-smothered sniveler. Little Bow. He'll hate you for the name when he grows up."

Lithia bridled her tongue, afraid to turn it loose.

"Well, the feast ends tomorrow," Keeta reminded. "And I hope that you are well enough to come out for the last day of fun. Because after tomorrow, the chieftain will call his conferences and get us whipped back into line again. Many things happen in his absence that have to be taken care of on his return, and not all of them are pleasant."

"I'm feeling ill again, Keeta. If you will be so kind as to go now and let me rest." With an effort of will, Lithia controlled the pressure in her chest. The stabbing of her heart seemed to swell with each beat.

"I'll check back later, Lithia, to see how you are feeling."

"Please, Keeta—I don't mean to be unkind, but people bother me; I am nervous yet. I prefer to be left alone."

"But I am your friend. Surely—"

"No, even you are not welcome."

"Well, if that's the way you feel!" Keeta flounced out.

"It is," Lithia called after her. "Please don't come back."

One more day. After tomorrow the chieftain would call his councils. Then he would know. All the pain of the past condensed into one unbearable pang. Lithia envisioned her baby being wrenched from her arms to meet his doom. She premeditated the terrible ache of emptiness, and without realizing she had done so, she gave a wild, inarticulate cry. Without her baby, life would be a path of thorns with no moccasins.

Now time had no meaning. Everything meshed together. The hours. The nights. The days. Then on the heels of the feast, a great lament began and the dirge echoed around the valley, growing in volume and intensity. Lithia's breath came in tight gasps of fright. Had word gotten out so soon? Was the death knell for her Broken Bow? She felt like an animal caught in a trap waiting for the trapper.

On trembling legs, she staggered to the door. "The mourning—what is it?" she called to a girl who rushed by.

"Haven't you heard?"

"No."

"Mamu is dead! She choked on the pemmican!" The girl wept. "Now she will not be here for me when I, yet an unfinished woman, need her."

"Mamu . . . dead? When did she die?"

"Sometime during the feast, they say. The chieftain is inconsolable. Some say she was his great-great-grandmother. Did you ever hear that?"

"No."

"Now what shall we do? Mamu was supposed to live forever and ever."

"Did she have her . . . her meeting with the chieftain before she died?" Lithia was hungry to seize on any detail that might bring hope.

"No. And that accounts for part of the chief's sorrow. How shall he know what went awry while he was gone? Mamu was his watchdog."

Relief swallowed Lithia. Though she stood motionless, she had the sensation of leaping. She had a few hours' reprieve.

Back inside the pueblo, she kissed Broken Bow again and again. He reached out his left hand and entwined it around her finger. She had never been happier. Whatever happened, today was theirs.

Chapter Five

The Proposal

"You're growing like a polliwog." Lithia nuzzled Broken Bow's neck. His cooing, a sound that needed no words of interpretation, warmed her heart. How the child filled his mother with delight!

She hummed cheerful lyrics to him as she kindled the fires in the clay oven or cleared away the ashes to lay her dough on the stones to bake. Each morning was a newly washed face, each evening a fresh pleasure.

Time ran with winged feet heedless of the dangers it created for Lithia and her rapidly growing son. She found ingenious means to normalize her life and his. She learned that she could go about her work as usual with Broken Bow tied in the cradleboard swinging from her back. In it he could not be distinguished from any of the other papooses. To Lithia, he *was* no different from other children; she seldom thought of his deformity at all.

She had tethered her fears and tried to forget about the curses. Therefore, when the chieftain appeared at her pueblo that morning, her mind froze into a solid block of panic. Who had told?

"You are a beautiful woman, Lithia," he said. "I owe a lot to your loss." He was a tall man and possessed the easy, high-headed dignity of his stature.

"Th-thank you." She shook so that the rattles attached to her son's cradle made a jingling noise behind her.

"You were not at the feast."

"No, your honor."

"I suppose that you were . . . confined with your child?"

"Yes, sir."

"I missed you."

The chief smiled. Lithia had never seen him smile. Indeed, she had never been close enough to him to notice that he had a handsome face and beautiful teeth. The spectacle surprised her. She took note of his firm body that rippled with muscles as Victor's had, and she suddenly felt ashamed that she had looked. A strange yearning stirred within her, a degree of feeling that gave her a jolt. She willed her eyes to turn away, but they would not obey.

"I've come to ask you to marry me. I have never had a squaw. In truth, I have never wanted one until now. I will bring you happiness—" he stopped to chuckle, "And a much larger pueblo. Winter comes."

To be in the arms of a man again . . . to be loved and protected . . . to share laughter and secrets. . . .

Lithia's face lighted and her eyes seemed full of sky. Victor once said she owned a passel of lovely smiles. She used one of them now as she impulsively moved her slender body toward the chieftain. He started toward her as eagerly. Then she remembered. A pain darted into the center of her heart, and the romantic moment lasted only that. If the chieftain had killed his own father, he would not spare her son, a child that was not his own flesh and blood. As much as she craved the embrace of a husband, she loved her son more. She could take no chances.

She pulled back and stiffened. "I . . . I cannot marry you," she stammered.

"And why not? Is there someone else?"

"No, my . . . my child . . ." the words died in her throat.

"He will grow up to be a great warrior. I will teach him the art of shooting a bow. He will be as my own son, strong and perfect of body. Like his father, the bravest of braves, no weakness shall haunt his soul."

Lithia's downcast eyes veiled her conflict. She stood mute and miserable.

"So what is your answer, pretty Lithia? Will you be my squaw?"

A war raged within; the woman of which Lithia was made cried out for understanding while the mother in her flashed a dread warning. She groped for a curtain of reserve to draw across her features, and finding none, she looked away to a clump of trees that stood sentinel in the distance. With her gaze averted, she whispered the word. "No."

"That is final?"

"I'm afraid it . . . must be."

"I am a proud man, Lithia. Too proud to beg. You know that I can have any woman in the tribe for the asking, but it is you that I want. I will not push myself upon a woman who neither loves me nor could walk beside me in harmony—" He turned away.

Lithia's heart twisted. "Wait! It isn't that—"

"You have reconsidered?"

"No, but . . ."

His eyes gradually released her, and he was gone without another word.

Lithia didn't realize that she was crying until she tasted the salt of her tears. *I cannot abandon my little Broken Bow. If only . . .*

Why had the gods cursed her? Why did Victor leave her to fight for the life of their child alone? Had he lived, he could have persuaded the chief to let their son live. Or they could have fled together to a place apart and secluded where Broken Bow would be safe.

After the chieftain's visit, days followed other days with a dull sameness. Like a spirit-wounded thing, Lithia limped through winter, gathering nuts and roots to sustain herself. Sometimes she joined other mothers around the campfires or beside the stream to wash her clothes. But the completeness that she felt before the chief's call was gone; at night, his features were etched on her thoughts long after she was in bed waiting for sleep.

As the months wore on, it became evident to Lithia that Broken Bow had been blessed with exceptional intelligence. He walked and talked at an early age, and the care he required generated the strength she needed for her busy days. The busier she was, the less time she had for regrets.

Although Keeta hadn't returned to Lithia's house, she followed Lithia about the village or in the woods, her eyes darting as fast as the tongue of a grass snake. "I saw the chieftain going to your pueblo, Lithia," she mentioned one day, folding her arms in a truculent posture. "I find that most extraordinary."

Lithia blushed a telltale red. "The chieftain goes wherever he wishes, Keeta."

"Oh?" Keeta's brows raised in an arch of accusation. "And he wished to come to you? All the squaws in the camp are talking, Lithia. It is not a good thing that is being thrown from mouth to mouth."

"They have nothing to say."

"When a single man goes to the pueblo of a husbandless woman, it bodes no good for that woman's reputation, be he chief or otherwise." Unspoken words hung in the air.

"I am guiltless of any wrong."

"Some of us believe that you are not innocent of enticing the chief—"

"I could have the chief if I wished, Keeta," exploded Lithia with white-hot anger. "But I have my reasons for not wanting to be married to him."

"He asked you?" Keeta's eyes saucered. "He asked you to *marry* him?"

Lithia nodded, a slow and reluctant nod.

"And you *refused* his proposal?"

"I did."

"Foolish, foolish you!" Keeta blasted. "Have you seen inside his pueblo?"

"I have not."

"It has *many* rooms: a room for each bed, a room for the table, a room for the oven. They say he had feathers plucked from birds to make his bolsters soft. Even his floors are covered with sheepskin. Would that *I* had your chance! I would marry him today! Are you crazy, Lithia?"

"I am." In her heart, she qualified her answer: *I am crazy about my son and I cannot let him die.*

"I knew it all along. It is fortunate for all of us that you chose not to be our chieftain's squaw. Although," she added, "I have my doubts that he even asked you."

Lithia tried to blot the future from her mind with the routine of daily tasks, yet time pulled her into the tomorrows, faster and yet faster. Broken Bow overgrew his cradle board, and then Lithia was obliged to keep him inside, away from prying eyes. She built a barricade across the doorway so that he could not get out.

With the child's active mind, keeping him amused

ate up Lithia's energy. She entertained him with childish games, occupying him so that he wouldn't miss the companionship of other children. As he grew older, they played the moccasin guessing game for hours: Lithia hid a piece of bone in one of three moccasins. Broken Bow tried to guess which shoe contained the bone. His infectious laughter filled the room, his spirit free and undaunted in spite of his missing hand. He was a happy child.

The boy loved stories. Bedtime tales graduated from fables to real life drama as Lithia whispered to him about his heroic father. The past, Lithia thought, almost had the flavor of fiction with Victor's face indistinct and dim. Time—and human forgetfulness—had impartially erased much of the pleasantry along with the hardships.

"Your father brought many fine skins," Lithia said. "He wanted his squaw and his papoose to have the best. He was honest and loyal; he never scalped a white man just for the pleasure of doing so.

"Nor would he drink the happy water made by the white man. He watched other braves stagger about, mistreat their squaws, and become crazed under the influence of the bad water. He said it made braves weak men and unfit for battle. When a man is full of whiskey, he is empty of sense."

"Tell me again about the thunderbolt, Mama," the boy requested night after night.

"Your father put himself between the chieftain and the fireball," Lithia told him. "It was our Victor who saved the life of the chief of the great Kotopaxi tribe." The mention of Victor's sacrifice still brought a tinge of bitterness to her voice and tears to her eyes. Yet Victor's son had a right to know of his heritage. He never tired of the story of the man he'd come to idolize in his growing mind. He asked endless questions, and with time and telling the answers came easier until the legend of a brave named Victor became a household classic. It was a pole star for the boy on black nights.

"Mama, will I ever have another father?" The question was innocent enough, but Lithia's answer came too quickly and with the same fierceness she used to push back memories of the chieftain's proposal.

"No!" Then she said it again, weaker and with a less harsh note. "No."

Every man child needed a father. It was unfair for a boy to know only the ways of a woman. But in the case of Broken Bow, there was no alternative.

The miracle was that somehow, from the quicksand of her own uncertainties, Lithia managed to give her son security.

Chapter Six

The Secret Told

Spring followed winter. Summer followed spring. Autumn came, then winter again. Days wheeled slowly by, and months rolled in the wake of days, each day a pattern of the others. Six times the seasons repeated themselves, and still Lithia guarded her secret.

She had eluded her child's destruction for this long, and she convinced herself that she would continue to do so with the unrealistic prospect that the future would somehow take care of itself. Why spoil the present with thoughts of a morbid tomorrow? Broken Bow knew nothing of the curses of the gods, so why borrow trouble?

In her wistfulness, Lithia reasoned that some release from the gods could be obtained in due time. If the gods had been determined to carry out their groundless grudge, they would have done so before now, wouldn't they? Employing this sanguine philosophy—and to stanchion her spirits—she sometimes lied to herself.

The years, however, had not relaxed Lithia's care never to let Broken Bow out of her sight for fear the chieftain might chance by. As long as the child learned nothing of the wretched curses, they could live peaceably for a long while to come, perhaps a lifetime. She considered inventing some anecdote to frighten Broken Bow so that he would dart out of sight if the chief should pass by. Yes, that's what she would do. . . .

Before she could get her story concocted, though, Broken Bow fell dreadfully ill, bringing on a whole new cycle of worry for Lithia. She dared not call the witch doctor. He would notice the missing hand and take the news directly to the chief. The illness might take away her child's breath and stop the beating of his heart, but the chief would never murder him.

Furthermore, the tactless doctor wouldn't hesitate to scare the child and then probe into the reasons he hadn't been abolished long ago. She recalled an incident in her early childhood when the dreadful man scared her with the gruesome faces and black bag. And with all his magic, he had not been able to keep her sick mother from an early death in the plague.

Lithia bathed Broken Bow's fevered body and stayed by his side. Great boils burst out on his skin, covering him. But Lithia rubbed them with ointment, filling him with purgative herbs. She rocked him, sang to him. And slowly, slowly, he began to mend.

He had never been a strong child like Keeta's husky son, but once more Lithia had saved him from death. A hysterical sense of relief swept over her. Did not this indicate that he was meant to live?

Lithia prided herself in her well-being. Oh, the tribal women dubbed her eccentric, and some even thought her mind had been affected by her husband's death. But let them think what they would as long as they left her alone. She had things well in command; Victor would be proud of her.

Broken Bow was fascinated with life and living. He loved every bug, every bird, every plant. He could identify the wild pea seeds and roots of elk thistle as well as Lithia could, and he helped her gather them. He watched with wonder as she separated strips of sinew for thread, and in a trice, he learned the process, assisting her with his deft left hand. She let him chew the edges of the skins to soften the leather so that the bone needle would go through it. Although his body was frail and weedy, his quick mind compensated for it. A charge of laziness could never be laid to the boy's account; he was skillful and industrious.

Colors especially delighted the child. He pleaded with Lithia to allow him to lay out the threads for the start of each new rug or blanket. "Did colors come down from the sky, Mama?" he asked. "They match the orange, scarlet, and purple of the evening. Or does the sky only reflect the colors of the wildflowers that bloom at the edge of the woods?"

She marveled at the depth of his perception and was not always able to answer his questions. "Your little mind is too big for me," she laughed.

With each new project, Broken Bow's excitement accelerated. "Oh, Mama, tell me!" he would beg. "What will the new blanket look like? Your rugs are the most beautiful things in this world! They look like a painted picture." He was content to sit with Lithia at the loom for hours, watching the patterns take shape under her nimble fingers.

"If I had more fingers, I could weave even faster than you," he said one day. It was the first mention he had made of his missing hand. "I could make a rug pretty enough for a god!"

One day when Lithia wasn't watching, he sat at the loom trying to make the thread go in and out with his one good hand. The threads became hopelessly tangled. Lithia thought to scold him, but he looked so woebegone that she couldn't bring herself to chide. "It isn't as easy as it looks, is it, my Bow?"

On hot days, Lithia moved the loom just outside the pueblo, insisting that Broken Bow stay inside. It was on one of these occasions that Keeta and her son, Slate, slipped up on hushed feet. Since no guests ever called on them, Broken Bow burst from the hut to stare curiously.

He couldn't take his eyes from Keeta. She had a thick black braid like his mother, but her eyes were different. They swiveled. And they weren't . . . lovely. She was shorter, heavier, and her face was not dressed in kindness. Along with his juvenile evaluation came a thankfulness that she wasn't *his* mother.

His attention traveled to Slate. This boy called Slate was much bigger than himself. He had strong arms, two perfect hands and appeared to be older. Broken Bow was suddenly seized with an inferiority complex; he turned shy and tried to hide behind his mother's skirts.

His movements only attracted notice to himself. Keeta stared in disbelief at Broken Bow's arm. "I . . . I . . . why hadn't I noticed before?" she gasped, registering shock. Did the chieftain not know about this boy? Why had he been allowed to live? And for six years? Could it be that Lithia was trading favors for her son's life?

Keeta, a woman who had experienced the brunt of the chieftain's hate for impaired things through one of her own children, felt the resurrection of an old, worn-out memory coming back to chafe her. *Her* child had been killed. Why should Lithia's child thrive? Her eyes blazed, then turned cold; her intimidating squint was like a pointed arrow.

Lithia moved between Keeta and her son, trying to divert Keeta's concentration from the boy's handicap. Even a "friend" could not be trusted, especially when there was a glint of malice in the depths of that "friend's" eyes.

Diligently Lithia focused on warding off the town gossip's questions. She changed the subject; she made trite conversation. And while thus distracted herself, she failed to notice that Slate had coaxed Broken Bow to play behind an outcropping of rocks nearby—away from the listening ears of both mothers.

The innocent child thought he had found a playmate in the burly son of Keeta. His eyes ready with welcome, he followed like a sheep to the slaughter, a stranger to unkindness.

When scarcely out of earshot, Slate, who was one summer older than Broken Bow, whispered menacingly: "You are not a good bow!"

Broken Bow looked bewildered and hurt.

Slate pointed to the arm with the missing hand. "See, you are broken. You are a bad, bad bow. And the chieftain kills bad bows like you."

Broken Bow studied his arm then looked at Slate in disbelief. A keening sound filled his throat, a wordless scream of defiance that failed to surface.

"It is true," vouched Slate. "Before me was a little brother who had sightless eyes. The chief burned his body to ashes so that the gods would be pacified. Someday soon he will burn you, too."

"My father gave his life for the chief of the Kotopaxi tribe. He took the thunderbolt in his belly." Broken Bow's shoulders lifted at a defiant angle, but his chin trembled. "My father—"

"Makes no difference what your father did," retorted Slate. "Our chief will have only the best in his tribe. Like me." He flexed his bronzed arms. "I shall be his strongest brave someday. I'm a *warrior*. Why, you couldn't shoot an arrow at a three-legged muskrat!"

"I can do lots of things with my good hand," defended Broken Bow, drawing himself to his full height.

"Hoot on! Nothing you say will save you. Why, our chief would even kill his own boy if he had a son like you. He killed his own father when he got old and crippled."

Like a beaver with sharp teeth, Slate's cruelty bit deeper. "Who named you, anyhow? Ask your mother. I dare say it was the witch doctor. You are cursed. The gods hate you. You shall die a horrible death!"

With the dastardly proclamation finished, Slate scampered back to his waiting mother, his damage to the sensitive-natured boy complete.

Broken Bow crept back into the pueblo, quaking. Waves of panic and terror raced through every part of his being. He hid his defective limb behind his back as the words of Keeta's son reverberated through his head. Could it be true that he was cursed of the gods? Or was this a cruel joke, an initiation trick that small boys played on each other to induct them into the sacred circle of tribal playmates? Slate did not blink an eye when he spoke; he made his words sting like a rawhide whip.

Lithia knew intuitively that something had happened, but she didn't know what. Broken Bow's black eyes didn't crinkle with laughter anymore. Instead, they were wide with terror. She worried about him; he ate none of the bread fritters she made for him from ground acorns. They were his favorite food, but nothing tempted him. He sat quiet and still in his silent world, sunk in an abyss of moody abstraction.

"What ails my Little Bow tonight?" she asked as the fire winked and flickered and then died away. With much maternal coaxing, Broken Bow spilled the story Slate had told him. The repeating came with bitter tears; deep gasping sobs wracked his thin body.

"How unkind of Keeta's son!" spat Lithia, trembling with temper, aware that her worst nightmare was just beginning. "You must forget the tales of that mischievous boy. He is only jealous because your one good hand is swifter than both of his. Because he is stronger and bigger—and whole—does not make him any better than you. The only benefit I can see is that it gives his mouthy mother something to brag about. *My son* is very special! His father was a courageous brave, and that's more than Keeta's son can say." She pulled Broken Bow into her arms and held him, willing to use any weapon against Slate's revelation.

"Did the witch doctor name me?" the boy asked.

"Of course not! Mamu, the tribe's revered midwife, gave you your nickname. And that was because she loved you. Your real name is Victor. You were named for your father and that name means *winner*. You will be a winner, you'll see!" She paused and narrowed her eyes. "Did that wicked son of Keeta tell you that the witch doctor named you?"

"Y-yes."

"See, he told a lie. The witch doctor has never seen you."

"But what about the chief, Mama? Does he really kill broken bows?"

Lithia could lie to anyone on earth but her own son. Nevertheless, she tried to deflect the shot destined to smite his heart by humoring him away from the dangerous subject. "Come now," she cajoled. "Let's forget evil curses, witch doctors, and mean chiefs." She took him by the shoulders and looked directly into his troubled eyes. "We have each other and remain unharmed to this day. What else matters?"

But deep inside, Lithia knew that since the secret had been told, life would never be the same for her or for Broken Bow. Worries writhed in her soul like vipers weaving their ugly heads for a deadly strike.

The wall she had tried to build around Broken Bow had come tumbling down. His world would never be quite whole again.

Chapter Seven

The Chief's Call

Keeta knew. And what Keeta knew the whole tribe would soon know.

The embryo of a terrible lie, a falsehood that might save her son, was already developing in Lithia's subconscious mind. All through the night, lying awake, she structured and polished the lie, and when the light from an invisible sun streaked the morning sky, she was ready.

She knew why the chieftain was at her door when he appeared. The plan, with frightening detail, unfolded before her. She was confident that it would work; she would stop at nothing to win.

The bear claws around the chief's swarthy neck bumped together with sinister foreboding; she tried not to notice them. Instead of a romantic smile, his lips wore scorn. It was like a blow to Lithia to see his nostrils narrowed and a scowl on his face.

Lithia had repeated the lie to herself so many times during the dark night that it almost seemed a cardinal truth to her. She'd found a few ounces of overlooked flint in her soul. She met her adversary at the threshold.

"It has been reported to me that you have given birth to a broken bow." The chief glared beyond her, his eyes in search of her child. The tone of his voice and the set of his jaw told Lithia that he had purposely forgotten Victor's act of bravery—and wished not to be reminded. "We have no broken bows in our superior tribe, only good bows. This is not my rule. It is an eternal law passed down from our ancestors, and it shall not be profaned. If you have borne such a son, he shall be destroyed this day."

Broken Bow still slept, and Lithia was grateful for that. She prayed that he might not awaken.

The chieftain respected the person of no living mortal, great or small. However, Lithia knew that he trembled in fear of the gods, and now she took advantage of that knowledge. It would require a carefully disciplined front to succeed in the great perjury. There could be no slips; her eyes must give no hint of the emotions that seethed behind them.

She took a deep breath and smiled. "The gods sent this broken bow to the mighty chieftain's superior tribe." It was a calculated, necessary lie somehow removed from dishonesty. It now stood as a supreme fact. "That is why I could not accept your noble offer of marriage." Again she smiled, using all the sorcery of her gender. Her child's only hope for survival lay in this enormous fake.

"The gods told me that I must not speak of my own role in the plan until you came today," she continued. "It would seem that I was boasting, you see. The gods called me to a special mission. My son is now six years old. I have six more years to prepare him for his work. The gods have informed me that on Broken Bow's twelfth birthday, he will become the finest bow of all. The gods are keeping his right hand in a golden casket, fashioning it into a magic hand for the chieftain's greatest battle. Even as Little Bow's father saved the chief's life, so shall his child. Surely, oh mighty chief, you would not think to destroy the very bow that will someday bring you your greatest victory! To bring death to him would surely bring death to yourself."

There, she had said it! It sounded good even to her own ears. Yet in spite of Lithia's confident declaration, the chieftain hesitated. His words would mean life or death for her son. Her heart turned to mush within her, but she dare not falter. Her eyes held their composure and covered her fabrication well. If she won, she would have a reprieve of six more years. With her breath postponed in suspense, she grew dizzy; the world spun, but she willed it aright again.

It was a monumental decision for the proud chief. Never had he allowed a defective human or animal to live. Never! He shot lame horses and made an immediate end to earth's halt and maimed. Yet if Lithia had encountered the gods as she claimed, the fury of the spirits would envelop him if he dispatched this child—and there would be no magic hand for him in the great battle of which Lithia spoke.

Besides, who would dare to lie to a chieftain? Not a mere woman! He searched Lithia's face, finding no trace of guilt in her countenance.

Could it be that the gods were indeed honoring the beautiful widow of brave Victor with a miracle child? The chieftain retreated into a deep silence and stayed there too long. The silence roared in Lithia's ears; she was sure her heart would stop beating any minute.

"And in what form did the gods appear to you?" The chief's question was as abrupt as it was unexpected.

Lithia had not anticipated the query, but her mind snapped into motion. Her son's life—and probably her own—hung in the balances. If the chief guessed that she was lying to him, they would both burn. Or hang. Or face an arrow.

She rebounded quickly. "In a vision, mighty chieftain. In the clear light of the morning." She closed her eyes as if reliving the vision. "The god who came to me was glowing. His eyes were the shape of diamonds, one emerald green and the other ruby red. Oh, but I was frightened! For I . . . a paltry mortal . . . had met with a . . . a being so . . . so *majestic*. And so powerful," she added, swaying for effect.

"I wonder why the god didn't come and tell me," the chief pondered aloud.

"You were not the one entrusted with the boy's care," she offered. "Gods appoint mothers as nurturers of infants. We know what to feed them and how to soothe their cries."

What if this unpremeditated answer did not suffice? The gripping fear would not release her, and she opened her eyes to find the chief's scrutiny glued upon her, his look hostile and intent. Her whole body grew weary from the encounter. What if his hatred for weaklings superseded his respect for the gods?

"You are not trying to deceive me, are you, Lithia?" He kept his shrewd eyes on her face.

"What woman in her right mind would ever do such a thing, O mighty chief? One who sees a vision or is blessed with a visit from another world can speak only the truth. It is a heavy load that I bear for you, your honor. The gods trust me, and I dare not break their trust."

"We shall wait." The chief's words fell like a boulder. "On the day of which the gods spoke, six years hence, if your son is indeed given his magic hand, I shall welcome him into the manhood of my tribe by changing his name. But if . . ." The chief turned on heavy heels and left the pueblo, taking his dire unfinished threat with him.

With the crisis now past, Lithia clutched Broken Bow and wept, praying to the gods although she doubted any assistance from a deity against whom she had dared to bear false witness. But why should she fear their curses now? No greater curses could come to her than those already conferred.

The tornado of apprehension blew itself out, and the wonder of what had just happened caught her in another whirlwind: one of wild elation. Six years was a long, long time; many things could happen in that interim. Perhaps the chieftain would be chopped down in battle; he had had many brushes with death in the past. Victor was no longer around to absorb the white man's fireball, and there was no other brave in the tribe so self-sacrificing. Or if the chief should become crippled himself, he could hardly impose on others a penalty of which he himself should be worthy. Or maybe a more powerful tribe would conquer, a tribe with a chieftain who made exceptions for unfortunate children. Oh, yes, many things could happen in the space of six years!

At least she wasn't attending the death ceremony of her son on this day. Hope was in the saddle again. The thought set her whole body at liberty, her relief as exaggerated as her earlier anxiety. A cloud of energy crackled about her, and she danced around the room feeling weightless inside and out.

Six years. Just now that seemed the equivalent of forever.

Chapter Eight

Across a Parching Trail

Conscience is an ulcer that gnaws at the vitals. The lie Lithia told was never still. It threshed and churned and gouged. No amount of self-justification could quiet its colic.

Months of fitful sleep and eating sparingly so that her son would grow strong left her physically bankrupt. Her neglect of her own spirit and body came to collect its wages. There were no resources in the bank.

When the illness struck, she hadn't the resistance to throw it off. The need for never-ending vigilance that had fueled her during Broken Bow's earlier years was no longer necessary; therefore, her willpower took a vacation.

A harvest had passed now since Broken Bow had encountered Keeta's son and felt the rejection of society. From that day on, none of Lithia's reassurances could restore the carefree innocence of childhood. A great oppression beset Broken Bow, and his eyes sparkled no more. He jumped at every noise.

The boy now moved about like a tracked animal who sensed danger but didn't know which direction to flee for escape. The hooting of the night owls frayed his delicate nerves; he had nightmares of cruel chieftains chasing him with a flaming torch to burn his body. He would awaken in a clammy sweat and lie awake for hours, trembling. He seldom went out into the sunlight, fearing an encounter with Keeta's son or the wicked chief. From dawn until dusk, he shadowed Lithia, a mute ghost of a child.

Lithia became tired and listless; her hands would no longer do what she told them to do. She tried to ward off the encroaching fever that tormented her, but it smote with a wracking intensity. Finally, she fell across the elk-skin cot and could not arise.

"It is not night, Mama," Broken Bow pointed out. "Why do you sleep while the sun yet shines?"

"I am sick, Broken Bow," she said. "But it is nothing; I will arise tomorrow."

But the next day she was no better. It seemed that she battled her way across many miles of burning thirst. She became disoriented; she had no idea how far she had come or how many miles she had left to go yet. She could neither stop nor turn around. The thirst was everywhere, consuming her.

She only knew that she must push on until the end of the parching trail of thirst was in sight. In her befuddled mind, she plodded on and on, stumbling, falling, picking herself up, and trying to focus her eyes on the objects ahead. Sometimes she confused the items in the pueblo with the imaginary, and everything swam in a sea of pandemonium. Always in her delirium Broken Bow was ahead, calling to her, and she was afraid to look back lest the chieftain be following at their heels. Horror piled on horrors, and her feverish chattering ended in long, heavy silences.

She could hear Broken Bow speaking from some-where a great distance away telling her that she would be better soon, but his words brought no comfort. When she tried to call his name, no words came. Her alertness was gone, and even her will to live faded, leaving her slack and empty. Each day the lassitude seemed more deadly than the day before. The black pit would swallow her forever once she fell in. The temptation to relax and let happen what would was almost overpowering.

Who started this terrible fire? Was it the witch doc-tor? Or Mamu? Or the chieftain? Or was it Keeta and those running feet? Would no one put the fire out and cool her aching head? Since she had withdrawn from the company of the neighboring squaws long ago, no one would come to check on her welfare. Alas, no one would know that she was ill! She was glad to be left alone, but what if . . . what if she didn't make it? What would become of Broken Bow? The gods . . . the magic hand . . . the chieftain . . . the lie . . . Around and around her thoughts circled.

"Shall I go for the medicine man, Mama?" Broken Bow bent over her.

A squeak of protest kept growling and swelling until it became a long, thin screech. "No! No, my son. Never!"

In the rational moments of her intense suffering, she pleaded with Broken Bow to tell no one of her plight. The witch doctor might uncover her lie and bring death upon them.

As Lithia grew weaker and weaker, Broken Bow, although only seven years old, sensed the seriousness of his mother's condition and his awesome responsibility to care for her. After all, hadn't she cared for him these many years? He had watched her make broth from roots and was sure he could do it himself. Behind the pueblo, the rich, dark earth produced an unlimited supply. When darkness gave him a sheath, he slipped out and gathered herbs by the moonlight.

Lithia had stored baskets of seeds, nuts, and dried onions along the plastered wall. These Broken Bow utilized, and when he ran low on meal, he ground more in the mortar, pushing the pestle with his left hand. Untiringly he worked, putting his own problems aside. His survival instinct worked overtime, and he would have found much fulfillment in his efforts had his mother not been so frightfully ill. He found that he could even make squaw bread, brown and lumpy. This he prepared for himself because Lithia was no longer able to swallow it.

If only his mother could live! Where would he hide if she died? How could he, so frail and so small, manage to bury her body beside his brave father as she would wish? Tears plagued his copper cheeks. Why wouldn't she answer him when he called to her? Something wasn't right about his mother. Her face was congested; her eyes saw nothing. It was no mere sleep that claimed her; she lay in a cave of apathy.

A hysteria seized him as she grew even weaker still; a devouring anxiety drove him on hour by hour, then minute by minute. Would she live until tomorrow?

When she finally opened her eyes, he had his question ready. "Could we pray to the gods to make you well, Mama?"

Lithia shook her head. "They . . . won't hear. . . ." she croaked. "I told a lie . . . once. They . . . hate me."

"Isn't there a God somewhere who would hear? Is there a God who wouldn't hate you?"

"I . . . don't know of . . . any. My son?"

"Yes, Mama?"

"I . . . must live. For you. Please don't . . . let me . . . die!" Lithia fell into a deep sleep, and when she awoke her eyes were clearer.

"You will live, pretty Mama." Broken Bow patted her head. It was damp. Did he imagine it or was her brow just a bit cooler than it was yesterday? He ran for the gourd bowl and held it to her lips.

"Here, sweet Mama, take this. While you were asleep, I slipped out to a place on the river where the water sings over the rocks and dipped good, cool water for you." Drop by drop he coaxed the liquid past her swollen lips and into her dry throat. She followed his instructions, not knowing or asking why. How much easier it would be to give in to the darkness that beckoned! Yet she fought it away, and after many painful days and nights, she began to recover.

The convalescence was slow. Only gradually did the hollows of her face fill out. She didn't look back, but she knew she had left the scorching trail behind.

Chapter Nine

The Great Stallion

The chieftain's horse had been struck by lightning, and he needed a replacement. He was most particular about his horses; in battle a man's horse could determine his victory or defeat. The animal must be large: at least seventeen and a half hands. But size played only a small part in the prerequisite. The chieftain couldn't have listed the precise requirements for the beast, but he knew he would recognize it when he saw it. . . .

It was on the autumn hunt that the chief found his horse. The hunt was going well, and he walked away from the hunters, bored with the embellished tales they exchanged. He had been restless since his talk with Lithia. Doubts leeched onto his mind like wood ticks, itching and irritating. He had hoped to make her his squaw—and the gods circumvented his plans by tying her up with a helpless child who was to have a magic hand. The chieftain didn't like his ideas thwarted even by "higher powers." He needed a wife, and five more years was a long time to wait. Too long.

As he strode along, mustering his thoughts, he abruptly stopped in his tracks. On the shoulder of a hill beyond, a band of wild mustangs ran with the wind. Their tails streamed out gracefully behind them; their manes lifted like tongues of fire in the breeze. What a magnificent sight! From behind a cover of heavy brush, he watched with bated breath as the symphony of snorts and pounding hoofs reached him.

Their exceptional size enthralled him; they were much larger than any he had seen in the white settlement. The white man's horses were spoiled; they weren't worth a spent arrow. They lacked speed and endurance. They were lazy, and he hadn't any patience for pampered steeds.

He watched the herd move across the plateau, dusting his hands together with satisfaction. Ah, how he would love to capture one of these wild things! They were tough and spirited.

He studied the animals individually. Although they were a matched lot, each had his own personality. What he wanted was a leader, a born leader. Some were followers; he didn't want a follower. He needed a stallion to complement his own disposition. Noiselessly, he slipped down onto the grassy knoll and marked their location. Not another soul must learn of his find.

At that instant, he spotted the special horse. His own muscles bounced and quivered with the animal's lissome movements. The horse was alert and sensitive but not easily spooked. His regal bearing said: *Don't challenge me; leave me alone.* Waves of hot excitement built in the chief. This was the horse he wanted, the horse he must have.

Day after day, the chief slipped away to his secret hiding place to watch the mustang. With each hour's observation, he was more infatuated with the animal. Then one day something happened that sent a surge of elation through him and demolished any shred of illusion: the wolves came. While the chief shaded his eyes against the morning sun to catch every detail, the other horses laid back their ears, stamped and grew agitated. *The* horse simply waited, unabashed. When the predators moved in on one of the colts, this horse seemed to know by instinct, with some third eye, that the wolves would work in a pair, one in front of the colt and the other behind.

The horse stepped behind the rocks, which hid him from view. When the wolves made their attack, the other horses ran whinnying away. The wolves followed the trail that led by the rocks as the horse seemed to know they would do. He was ready. When the attackers came by, the horse sprang upon the wolf that was following behind to hamstring the colt. With a slashing of hooves, the horse killed the enemy then turned on the remaining wolf and drove it from the herd, wounded and dying.

The chief was beside himself. A mustang who could outfox a wolf—and with such bold courage—must be captured at any cost.

He devised various means of trapping and capturing, but the mustang was too smart for him. When the hunt ended, he returned to the tribal camp empty-handed and disappointed. His disappointment, however, was seasoned with admiration, and he was more determined than ever to have that horse for his own. No other would do. What enemy could ever defeat the two of them, an indefatigable beast and a cunning rider?

The chief's chance came during the winter. The snow fell in massive drifts, the worst "ghost face" in the tribe's history. Through the deep snow, the chieftain made his way to the hill from which he had often watched his horse. The relentless flakes had covered the animals' food source, and they were trapped in a canyon and hungry. This was the opportunity he awaited.

Singling out the one mighty horse, the chieftain started toward him, but the horse moved away with powerful strokes, clearing a path in the snow. It was hard for the chieftain to believe the impossible distance the horse traveled in his emaciated condition. Patiently, he followed until the stallion became winded.

When at last he had gained enough ground to approach the horse, the chief offered feed from the bag of grain he had brought. With malignant contempt in his eyes, the proud stallion refused to eat. His stubborn dignity delighted the chief.

Each morning the chief brought food and each morning the horse ignored the hand that held it. Then the temperature dropped, and ice crusted the snow. Some of the weaker horses died while the others hovered close to starvation. When the indomitable mustang grew too weak from malnutrition to resist, the chief ground and heated grain, making a mushlike mixture, and forced it down the horse's throat.

For many days the chief coaxed food into the unwilling mouth of the great stallion until at last the horse recognized and responded to his master. "Aha! The win is worth the war," crowed the chief. "I've never seen finer horseflesh." He put a rope about the animal's neck and led him back to the camp with utmost ostentation.

They were two of a kind, inseparable—the chief and his horse. Each acknowledged the other's invincibility, and under the grueling training of a war horse, this one never flinched. He seemed to understand the purpose for which he was chosen and came to relish his calling. The chieftain had the witch doctor pronounce blessings upon his new steed. Surely no chief had ever sat astride such a horse!

The mustang was the envy of every Indian brave who saw him. Bonded together as one, horse and rider presented a fearsome sight.

No one but the chieftain had ever sat on that broad back; the chieftain declared it would remain that way forever. But what the chieftain did not know was that someday there would be a second rider . . . someone he least expected.

Chapter Ten

Unwanted News

"I have a craving for wild berries." Lithia pulled herself to a sitting position. "They will purify my bloodstream and make me strong again. I wish they were ripe."

"They are ripe, sweet Mama. Your mind has been lost with your illness for many days, and we are in the season of fruit and flowers now."

"I am not yet able to go and pick."

"I will go into the woods and gather some for you." Broken Bow welcomed the light in his mother's eyes. Whatever she wished, he would get for her.

"But you cannot go into the forest alone!"

"Why not? Nothing will harm me." The boy spoke with more mettle than he felt; under no other circumstances would he leave the safety of the pueblo.

"You will be very careful?"

"As the gods listen, I give you my promise."

Lithia looked deep into the boy's eyes. Before her

brush with death, she found fear there. Now there was a new quality. She couldn't name it, but it spoke of maturity. He wasn't quite a child now though not yet a man. Somewhere they had traded places. She had once been his lifeline; now he had become hers.

She nodded. She did need the fresh fruit. "Don't dally in the woods and bring a worry upon my head."

"You have no worries."

Broken Bow had been gone only a few minutes when Lithia heard the moccasin-shod feet stop at her door. "Lithia?" Keeta's face filled the doorway, blotting out the sunlight.

"Yes?"

The woman's eyebrows shot up in surprise when she saw Lithia's wasted body. "You . . . are ill?"

"My road leads me back to a better day," replied Lithia.

Keeta looked around intrusively. "Your son is . . . gone?"

"Yes."

She searched Lithia's pale and drawn face. "Then it is grief."

"Grief?"

"I know how you feel, Lithia. I have walked in your moccasins. You were but a girl when it happened, but surely you remember when the chief massacred my own son who was born without sight."

"Yes, I remember. But why should you dredge up that terrible thing today?"

"I mention it to let you know that what you have gone through is no more than what I went through myself. I am offering sympathy. I'm sorry that the chieftain killed your son, but you were permitted to keep him longer—"

"I don't know what you are talking about, Keeta. The

chieftain didn't kill my son."

"You said he was gone."

"He went into the woods to pick berries. I hungered for fruit and he has gone to get some for me."

The smug pith left Keeta's features. "Oh, I see. Then why drips your flesh from you?"

"An illness has just passed over."

"I don't understand. I know that the chieftain came to your pueblo, Lithia, after I told him—" she caught herself. "That is, I saw him come here about a harvest ago. Why did he not kill your imperfect child?"

Lithia was afraid to lie again. She had scarcely escaped the wrath of the gods with her life because of the last untruth. So she sidestepped with a half-truth. "He made an agreement with me," she said. "I can keep my son for a few more years."

"In return for personal favors?"

Lithia's face turned crimson at Keeta's inference. "Absolutely not!"

"Then why should he give you many years to enjoy your son when he took mine at once? That is favoritism—"

"Did your husband give his life for the chief?" Lithia flung the question at Keeta, hitting a sore spot. "He still honors Victor."

"So that's it?"

Lithia dropped the matter into a pool of silence and let it sink. She would not allow Keeta to push her over the brink into the pond of dishonesty.

"And did he ask your hand in marriage again?" Keeta goaded.

"No."

"Of course he didn't," Keeta gave a snort of laughter. "And he won't ask again. You know, don't you, that he has taken himself a squaw?"

Why that knowledge should bother her, Lithia didn't know. But it did. She was afraid to take the top layer of skin from the pain of the revelation to look deeper, afraid of what she might find beneath. "I didn't know," she said, fumbling with her coverlet.

"You missed the chance of a lifetime," taunted Keeta. "I can't imagine why he didn't ask *me*. I would have given my turquoise necklace for the chance you had. *I* would have been a perfect wife for him. I could have kept him well informed on all the tribe's activities. My son would have adapted princely. But it is too late now for you *or* me."

"Have you . . . seen her?"

"Only from a distance. I saw her coming from the chief's pueblo this morning. Those who have met her say that she is a most beautiful woman."

"Is she one of our tribe? Someone I would know?"

"No, she isn't from our village. They say the chieftain went to a northern camp and fetched her home with him. Her name is Essence. Some say she is an older woman and that she had a husband before. Rumor has it that she may be too old to bear sons for the chieftain, which means a successor will be chosen from the boys of our tribe. My Slate would be an excellent choice."

"I suppose the chief loves her."

"They say he's quite fond of her. But I must say, Lithia, you seem to have a more than common interest—"

Lithia squirmed. A pain stabbed her heart, but she couldn't tell if the hurting was real or abstract. "Thank you for coming, Keeta. My strength wanes. You may return when I am stronger, but you must leave your unwanted tidings behind." She grew so bold that her eardrums pounded with blood. "And reporting my son to the chieftain or his squaw will avail nothing. Be assured that he knows all about Broken Bow and his missing hand!"

Chapter Eleven

Meeting in the Woods

Whispers and sighs feathered through the trees, making the forest a curious and exciting place to Broken Bow. Mysterious life announced itself from hundreds of throats as the wildlife exchanged greetings.

He had never been farther from camp than the river. That would change today, for today he planned to go deep, deep into the woods for the choicest of berries.

The doeskin boots that Lithia had made for him were soft and giving, light as air. He could feel the earth through them, warm and spongy. The heat of the ground ran up through his legs into his body. A giddy sense of freedom—as if he stood at the very core of life and felt its heartbeat—gripped him, bringing a thrill he had never experienced before. He was as free as the wind in the woods, suddenly one with his surroundings. Here was a whole world waiting to be explored.

He was at once unshackled from the nagging fears and mental tortures his young heart had borne for so long, loosed from the curses of frowning gods and an unkind chief, and liberated from the threat of his mother's death. When a ray of sunlight splashed across his chiseled face, he cherished its caress and laughed aloud.

As his ink-black eyes drank in the glory of the wilderness, he talked to it. "You almost make me forget my errand," he said. "My mother reminded me to hurry home with her fruit." This self-prompting gave his ego a boost; he was on a mission that required dependability. He was now grown up and important, the man in charge at his house.

His mother had also warned him to keep his bearings lest he become lost. Some boys, she said, wandered into caves and never returned. He'd steer clear of all caves. He put mental marks on jackknifed trees and unusual rock formations as guideposts. This was an ingenious system that nobody had ever thought of; he was immensely proud of himself for thinking of it.

Had he ever been so at peace with the world, at peace with his own heart? He hoped that his mother needed berries often so that he might come to this intoxicating place again and again. The *smells* . . . He loved them. They touched the quick of his being: the damp wood smells, the resin of the pine, the clean scent of burbling water.

He measured himself against the height of a towering pine, but that made him feel overwhelmed and small. Best it would be to stand by a willow that made him feel taller. He peeled the bark from a twig with his teeth, tasting the green bitterness. It cleaned his mouth and cleared his nose.

Above the tops of the branches, a frail cloud moved across the morning sky. *Surely there must be a Great Spirit somewhere,* Broken Bow mused. *Someone who made the trees and stones and bubbling streams. If there is such a One, He is good—better than any of the gods on the totem pole. A God who made such a fabulous world would wear a smile instead of a scowling face. . . .*

Broken Bow looked up, trying to locate that Someone. He felt a stirring inside and suppressed an urge to shout, "I love you, Great Spirit!" The idea made him tingle all over.

When he came to the winding skein of river, he removed his boots and waded in, letting the cool ripples roll over his feet. The sun, gleaming on the pebbles in the water, turned them to multicolored jewels. But lifted from the stream bed, the rocks became smooth and faded. A turtle plunged into the water from its basking place on a log, causing Broken Bow to throw back his head and chuckle with boyish abandon. However, when a water snake slid by, he scrambled from the brook. Snakes were bad omens, and goodness knows, he and Lithia had had enough bad luck in their lifetime!

Across the creek, he was in virgin territory. There was no path now, only crisscross trails made by animals going to water. Coming upon a baby bird that had fallen from her nest and injured her wing, he murmured, "Little broken wing, I know how you feel. I am broken, too." With utmost care, he placed her back in her low nest.

He had stopped to watch a squirrel when an inner voice reminded him of his reason for coming to the woods. The berries . . . He should be looking down instead of up. He would find no berries in the treetops. Hastening his steps, he came to a small opening proliferating with ripe dewberries. How plump and perfectly formed they were! He gave a cry of delight. The gods had smiled on them, giving them a special beauty this year. Or had that special God put them here just for Lithia? Doing something nice for somebody would be characteristic of Him.

Wouldn't his mother be pleased? And wouldn't she

enjoy his stories? He held the bowl he had brought from the pueblo between his ribs and the semi-arm as he knelt among the vines. The berries stacked higher and higher, and the bowl was almost filled when Broken Bow heard the cracking of a limb. He whirled around.

What he saw first was the shadowed bulk of a horse. He had never seen such a huge beast. Its powerful front legs looked like tree trunks. They were painted with zigzag stripes that made him dizzy when he tried to follow them with his eyes. Red circles were painted around the stallion's ears.

This was war paint! The rider was either going to or returning from a battle. The horse's tail gave another clue; it was braided and tied in a knot with eagle feathers woven into the braid. Broken Bow knew enough about the tribe's hallowed customs to know that this horse was ornamented for warfare, and the painting on his hind quarters showed that he belonged to someone highly regarded. *Someone from his own tribe.*

The awe-struck boy had little time to think. He turned his eyes upward until they met a broad, painted face topped with blue-black hair, hair that had been coated with bear fat until it shone. The chieftain!

Broken Bow's heart beat a sharp staccato, and he wanted to cry out for his mother, but no voice came. The terror that had lived in the lining of his stomach all these months now had a tangible shape, and that shape sat on a horse in front of him. His breath hurt as it made its way into his lungs.

The chief's face might have been hewn from stone. It was hard, graven with scorn. His lips locked in a cruel line, and a growl rose low in his throat. Slowly and deliberately, he fitted a long, spiked arrow—pointed at one end and sporting an eagle feather on the other—into the giant bow. Then he aimed it directly at Broken Bow's head.

In his fright and confusion, Broken Bow dropped the bowl of berries and started to dart away into the brush. But no, he must not do that. He would be a running target. The chief would waste no time in killing a coward. If die he must, he would die bravely. For his ailing mother he had come away from the pueblo today, and he was willing to give his life for her. He stood unmoving, almost strangling in his effort to keep still. It seemed that a hand had seized him by the throat so that he couldn't breathe. Oh, if he only knew whom to call for help in time of trouble! *Oh, Great Spirit, help me!*

What happened next Broken Bow could not remember clearly. From somewhere a crazed boar lunged at the horse on which the chieftain sat just as the chieftain prepared to release the shaft. He was obliged to use the ready arrow to kill the fierce animal instead of Broken Bow. When the arrow was spent, the chief goaded his horse and raced away into the woods.

Broken Bow's legs wobbled and his feet wanted to fly across the ground, but he did not run. The temptation lasted only a moment. Hadn't he come into the woods for berries for a sick mother? He would accomplish his purpose or perish in the trying. His mother was depending on him.

Slowly he stooped to pick up the spilled fruit and return it to the bowl from which it had fallen. Lithia would have fresh berries today.

"The gods saved you from the chief's arrow," Lithia vowed when Broken Bow told her the story. But that didn't make sense to Broken Bow. Why would the gods save him? If he was under their curses as Keeta's son had pointed out, why should they care whether he lived or died? Surely they would prefer that he meet his death there in the woods rather than be a continued nuisance to them.

"I see that the chief's word cannot be trusted," Lithia said. Broken Bow noticed that there were shadows like bruises beneath her eyes.

"What word, Mama?"

"Never mind. But you must never, never go into the woods again."

"Only if you need berries," he said, his chin lifted. From now on he must do things with a man's determination and responsibility. He—and some Great Unseen Spirit—had pulled Lithia through the black and awful valley. What else mattered?

Chapter Twelve

Slate's Plan

Keeta's son, Slate, stepped from his mother's dwelling into the predawn air. A warm draft of dew-laden earth came pleasantly toward him, the spirit of spring borne upon its breath. He stretched his legs and looked around. Within his breast was a stone of discontent. He was restless. Restless, and often irritable. Why must he wait until his twelfth birthday to be initiated into the tribe's sacred society of manhood?

He made a fist and flexed his arms. His muscles rivaled most of the warriors' biceps. He could outshoot any of them already; his hunting ability stood toe to toe with the best. No tree was too tall for him to climb, no cliff too high to scale. An ill-natured mirth beetled his brow. He could hardly wait to lift his first pelt of light-colored hair and bring a dripping scalp back to the tribal camp. Wouldn't the other young braves drool?

Each time the chieftain rode by on his stallion, the twain as one, Slate coveted both, the chief's position and his horse. The chieftain had saluted him on several occasions. Nothing had been said, but the look left nothing unsaid. *He has aspirations for me,* Slate thought. *Perhaps since he has no sons . . .*

Slate was glad that winter's back was broken and warm weather loomed ahead. He always rushed the seasons because he had many ambitions for the future. He planned to build a larger pueblo for his mother with his own capable hands; he had already begun to collect materials. His scheme was to have the best dwelling in the village—and the most lavish totem pole anywhere, with all the gods grimacing from it.

The gods had certainly made him what he was: strong, smart and self-sufficient. He must be careful to pay homage to each of them, slighting none. He would continue to pray to them before any decision he needed to make. When he reached the top in the tribe, he would see that the entire tribe revered them, too. Any dissenters would be killed; he would be even more religious than the present chieftain.

The golden edge of the sun swam up from the horizon through bars of crimson. It seemed to cling to the top of a tall pine tree. He turned slowly in a half circle and looked toward the pine in the west where the sun would set, hanging for a moment in that tree, then leaving streamers of purple and gold as it went out for the night. Slate had learned to tell time by these two trees. They marked off the inner boundaries of the tribal domain, a domain that someday would be his.

It had rained during the night, bringing out the earth's perfume and leaving little puddles here and there. He snuffed the cool of dawn, nibbling at it with his nose and licking at it with his tongue. That was one thing for which his tribe could be grateful: they lived in an area of plentiful rainfall.

The valley rose to a new day. As daylight seeped in, it transformed everything from black to gray, from gray to pink, then from pink to a magic yellow gleam of sunshine. The hour was early and the tribe dull with sleep yet, but Slate was bursting with pent-up energy. He raised his arms toward the wide expanse of sky and darted like a roe down the path led by the pueblo of Lithia and her one-handed son. There was no movement or sound there. He mouthed an oath at the dwelling.

In the woods on this March morning, a marvelous plan began to formulate in Slate's mind. He had pondered for many days upon a means to elevate himself in the chieftain's grace. The chief had no sons, and someday the position would be passed to someone else. Why not himself? He considered himself the most important, most interesting person in the tribe. Who would be a likelier candidate?

It must be admitted that Slate's father had not been a renowned brave. Actually, he had met an infamous death when he fell from his horse and hit his head on a stump, a victim of his own drunkenness. He was not afforded a colorful burial. But that was one of the chief's premier traits: everyone was an individual with him; every man had his own personal merits. No skeleton in the closet could add to them or subtract from them. A son was not held accountable for the blunders of his witless father nor a son honored for the deeds of a brilliant parent.

Take that milksop of a boy called Broken Bow, for instance. His father had been given a fine send-off for his bravery in saving the chief from the white man's bullet. But Broken Bow had not benefited from the honors of brave Victor, had he? What, by the way, ever happened to the handless dullard? He hadn't been seen for many a moon. Had the chief destroyed the boy secretly? Usually, such a killing was made public, and the whole tribe showed up for the execution. Why had the weakling been allowed to live in the first place? *I'll ask Mother about it,* Slate decided. Keeta would know. She knew about the affairs of the whole Kotopaxi community. *He* should know what was going on in the tribe if he were someday to be the . . . uh . . . er . . .

The plan added dimensions as Slate ran along the silvery thread of a stream. The sun glanced off the surface of the water in a thousand sparks of light, but the rays of glory that flashed across its surface paled against Slate's luminous plan. He would find the finest of wood and make the most elaborate totem pole ever seen by human eyes! Then he would present it to the chief when he was initiated into the mighty Kotopaxi tribe as a junior brave.

He had several months yet to complete the project. "It will require many, many hours of hand carving," he said aloud, "for it must be perfect. Ha! No gift would please the chieftain more. Nothing would make a greater impression. Nothing will better help me reach my goal." The ghost of a smile haunted his lips.

Keeta took note of her son's animation when he returned for breakfast. Slate was her pride and joy. He had something up his sleeve: something wonderful and worthy. She suspected that it had something to do with his future in the tribe. He'd thirsted for command since his cradle-board days.

She could almost be thankful that Slate's slow-thinking father was dead so that no shadow would be cast to darken the stardom of her exceptional son. There was no telling to what heights Slate's ambition would lead him. Why, someday she might be the blessed mother of the *tribal chief;* that would be next best to being *married* to a chieftain. She hugged the delightful thought to herself.

Slate's long absences from home were never questioned as he worked laboriously on his pole. In her vaporish cloud of imagination that had gone amuck, Keeta envisioned her son in secret rendezvous with the chief, being groomed for the lofty office. These training sessions would surely bring a special comradeship between Slate and the chieftain. As long as her son's eyes burned as brightly as a campfire, she was happy with whatever occupied his time. Someday he would reveal his guarded secret to her, and she would be selective with whom she shared the secret. She'd try not to let it out of the Kotopaxi tribe!

Slate's hands wore blisters from the long hours of whittling. Keeta mistook the blisters for the price of intense archery practice—with the chief himself as Slate's teacher, of course.

Faces took shape on Slate's pole, awful and contorted faces. Disagreeable as they were, they were nonetheless perfectly configured. Slate's talents lay in sculpturing, and it appeared that the totem pole would be finished in plenty of time for the initiation. Just a few more weeks to go . . .

Pride swelled Slate's chest. His mother gave his overweening vanity a hoist every day. "You will be the brave who will take the chieftain's heart away," she predicted. "He has no sons, and I have seen his eyes drinking of you lately."

It was hard for Slate to keep his secret from Keeta. But in her motherly doting, she would spread the word like a fire gone rampant, and Slate wanted his gift to be a surprise. One thing about his mother, she had never been able to hold her tongue. He smirked. She would have the news of his becoming chief announced before the witch doctor could sneeze!

"I hope that you are right in your prophecy, my wise mother," Slate beamed. "I am devising a gift that will please the chief better than anything in the world. Just you wait and see!"

"A headband!" she guessed.

"No."

"Boots?"

"No."

"I can't guess, Slate."

"You must wait and see."

Waiting was Keeta's most difficult chore, but she sighed with content. "The gods sent me a chief in waiting," she boasted. "How could I be so lucky?"

"By the way, wise mother, what ever happened to the boy with the hand all gone? Lithia's son?" Slate threw in abruptly. "He seems to have disappeared. Often I pass by Lithia's pueblo and have called to the boy, but I get no reply. Is he yet alive?"

Keeta scowled. The mention of Broken Bow made her angry. "Yes, he lives still. I do not know how or why. I make calls on Lithia now and then just to see if her fragile son is still breathing. She avoids my eyes and won't discuss the subject of her son with me at all. I believe that she is hiding some evil thing in her heart. I'm beginning to suspect that she may have lied to the chieftain—"

"*Lied* to the chieftain? But, my wise mother, *no one* would lie to the mighty chief of the Kotopaxi tribe."

"Lithia is very deceptive."

"If you suspect this, then shouldn't we report it?" Slate had a sudden inspiration that such a disclosure might advance him farther in the chief's estimation.

"Perhaps we should, but first let me see what I can learn—"

"If that Broken Bow has not been disposed of by the time I take my place as chief, I shall not waste another minute in doing my duty, for I shall keep the Kotopaxi tribe pure." His lips pinched down to a cruel line, and he spoke with fluent violence. "My rules on weaklings shall surpass the chieftain's. His rule does not include *women* who become crippled. I say a tribe needs good, strong squaws like my own wise mother to produce flawless braves. I will make *no* exceptions."

"But my son, what if *I* should—"

Slate had sped away. He returned to his hideout in the woods to put the finishing touches on his beloved treasure, the pole that made the gods look alive. The chief would find it irresistible! A wild, mirthless laugh broke from his throat. Nothing could stop him now!

However, upon reaching his destination, Slate looked about frantically. Was he in the right place? What was amiss? Where was his totem pole?

He strove for control, numbed by the futility that invaded his spirit. The shavings were there, but his pole was *gone*. His shoulders folded with dejection. He would not have time to carve another before the upcoming ceremony.

Chapter Thirteen

The New Squaw

Keeta's curiosity—and her penchant for scattering scandal—took her to the chieftain's pueblo to see the new squaw there. She had not met her personally, and it was time that she had some new twaddle to twitter.

Essence didn't socialize much; she was seldom seen outside the "palace" and did not accompany the chieftain on his tribal calls. She seemed to be content to be a turtle in her own shell. Keeta found the woman baking bread. A subtle smell of sweet spices filled the room.

"I came for a chat," announced Keeta.

"You came to see *me?*" Essence asked, surprised.

Essence was, true to the reports, a beautiful woman. Her eyes, set in webs of finely wrinkled skin, gave the odd effect of other eyes behind those one saw. A delicious bloom of womanhood lay not so much upon her skin as inside it; the air around her took on a sheen that was there but wasn't there. Keeta had been unprepared for the phenomenon of a person with such an aura. Essence fascinated her.

"I came to meet the new squaw in our village," Keeta said, wishing to open the conversation with pleasantries. "I'm sure the chieftain is glad to have someone to cook for him."

"Yes, indeed," Essence gave a silky laugh. "He makes *dreadful* johnnycake!"

"I am Slate's mother, Keeta."

"Oh, yes! That's the boy the chief has his mind set on for training, isn't it? It takes a good man to maintain the delicate balance of care and discipline to keep so large a tribe happy. The chief says your son will likely be the number one brave of the next generation. I'm honored to meet his mother."

Keeta preened. Her crowning ambition was to see her son sitting on top of the heap. "Without a doubt my son is chieftain material. He has a true eye for shooting, fast feet for running, and sure *hands* for the bow." She emphasized the word *hands*.

"But what of his heart? I tell the chief that he must begin to look on the inside, too."

"What do you mean?"

"The outside of a person is only the shell that holds the real man inside. Kindness must be the native climate of one's soul. Is your son kind to others? Is he courteous? Is he honest?"

Keeta's forehead puckered, but she quickly transmitted her frustration into aggression. "Why, most certainly!"

"I say that the inside is much more important than the outside. The gift of goodness is rare indeed. One can be big on the outside and little on the inside, or little on the outside and big on the inside. A spring cannot be judged by its size but by the sweet water that flows from it, don't you see?"

"Oh, my son, Slate, is fearless inside! Why, he can hardly wait to get his first scalp!"

"His first scalp?" It seemed that Essence didn't understand.

"He hopes that he may harvest as many scalps of the white man as our illustrious chieftain has. He talks about it often—and I can see the dream in his eyes when he mentions it. By the way, where does the chieftain keep the scalps that he has taken? I had hoped that he might have them on display so that I might see–"

Essence's grave expression, undefinable, stopped Keeta midsentence. Was it sadness that roosted in Essence's eyes? Or anger? Or remorse?

"The scalps are not . . . here," Essence said. "I insisted that the chief remove all of them before I came. That was one of the conditions of my living here. In my tribe, we lived in peace with the white man. He gave us books and tools and new kinds of seeds in exchange for our furs. We were friends. My former husband never scalped a white man. They were our neighbors, and we cared for one another. We even had feasts together. I cannot accept violence against another person. Another's way of life may be different from mine, but it is just as valuable, nonetheless.

"Warring is not the way to winning. War only brings death and bloodshed. We learned much from the white man's missionary. He taught us to live in harmony with all men and to treat others as we would wish to be treated ourselves. It makes the heart be still.

"The chieftain doesn't see it my way—and I don't know that he ever will—but he must hide the killing and the scalps from me if I am to be happy here and if I am to keep cooking his favorite johnnycake!"

Keeta didn't like this kind of talk. Some premonition passed over her mind like a dark wing. She took the verbal reins of the conversation and steered it away from the dangerous precipice. "You have a lovely pueblo," she said, letting her eyes take in the details for repeating. "And most lavishly furnished."

"Yes, the chieftain likes his comforts when he comes home. And he rightly deserves them, for he does work tirelessly for his tribe."

"You were from a different tribe?"

"Yes, I was married to an Ayutook chieftain who . . . died."

"And you had no children?"

For a moment a candle seemed to burn behind Essence's face; then over the light swept a shadow. "I had two children," she said. "They were washed downriver in a flood, and I never found them. I suppose the Great Spirit needed them elsewhere." Her fingertips came together, seeking out the shape of prayer.

"And you will have no more children?" Another child—one born to the chieftain—would wreak havoc to Keeta's plans for her own son.

Essence's smile bleached. "You ask many questions. That answer I do not know. Who can know? Someday I might adopt a motherless papoose. But at my age, I would not be as serene as a young mother to endure a baby's many cries. I fear I would cry myself!"

"How old are you?"

"I have seen more than forty summers. But why do you ask about things that don't concern you?"

"My mind searches to know everything," Keeta said without recoil.

"It is not good," Essence said.

"Sometimes it is. You wrap yourself in your pueblo and don't know what goes on about you—even the things you should know." There, she'd thrown out the hint about Lithia.

"I can't imagine what I should know that I don't know about this camp. The chieftain tells me what is necessary, and I am here for him. I am happy and cared for. What else is important?"

"But what would you say if I should tell you that a younger woman is trying to entice the chief away from you?"

Essence tilted her head and laughed. "Ah, if anyone pursues the chief, he will flee! I know what the man is made of. If there are advances, it will be he who makes them and none else."

"I have seen it! The whole tribe knows. The chieftain visits the pueblo of the widowed squaw named Lithia."

"That's the pretty squaw with the broken bow?"

So Essence knows about Lithia's child. "Yes. She has no scruples."

"Ah, I am sorry for her if the gods fail to keep their end of the bargain! The chief has a ridiculous rule about the weaker of humanity. I don't agree with him. If he would but look on the *inside.*" She signed. "The woman's son may have a brilliant mind. I'm glad my deceased husband had no such rule. Indeed, it is foolish. Charity is the sinew that holds any civilization together. When charity is lost, all is lost."

"Spare your pity for Lithia," Keeta said with a malicious sneer. "She is working behind your back."

"She turned down her chance to marry the chief before I came."

"Are you not jealous of her?"

"Why should I be?"

"And if she should steal the chief's affection from you?"

"I suppose that I should then move to her pueblo and she to mine."

"Without bitter feelings?"

Essence gave an uncertain nod. "My dear lady, I want only the chief's happiness. He has been in love with the beautiful squaw since her brave saved his life. No one knows that better than I. But she spurned his love, and now it is I who cook his johnnycake."

"You knew that when you came?"

"No, but I soon learned. He told me all."

"Then why do you stay?"

Essence's eyes twinkled. "I cannot go and let him bake his own *dreadful* johnnycake, can I? He *needs* me; that's why I stay."

"He will not take more than one wife?"

"It is against his principles."

If the chieftain confided everything to his squaw, then there was something Keeta must know. "Why does the chieftain let Lithia's brokenbodied child yet live? I am aware that the boy's father saved the chief's life, but there isn't any resemblance between father and son. The child is but a leaf. His father was an oak—a dark brown trunk of a man whose arms could truly be called limbs. He had two hands as strong as granite. Why—?"

"The chieftain says there is an agreement with the gods."

"Whose agreement?"

"Lithia's. And I hope that she wins! I cannot abide the murder of innocent children. But the chief is unbending in his decisions. No woman will tell him what to do. Not even I." She seemed to feel that she had said too much. "Oh, I'm not implying that the chief is a brute! He is good even though he is wrong headed in some areas. His great strength is his honor; his one weakness his dishonor. He is an arrogant man and hard, but with someone he loves, he is different. Deep inside runs a vein of gentleness; he has a soft mouth and warm eyes. He would have made a kind and loving husband for the woman of whom you speak. I am sorry that she could not accept his proposal although it would have barred my coming."

"Tell me about Lithia's contract with the gods."

Any friendship with Keeta was bought with gossip and more of it, and Essence had no desire to purchase such fellowship. "I shall not tell you. Since I did not hear it for myself, that would be hearsay." Her eyes accused Keeta. "I have no use for *nosy* squaws. And if your son, Slate, has your characteristics, I shall advise the chieftain—" Her look held her victim.

"Slate has never minded another's business in his life!" defended Keeta, fighting a seizure of anger. She must tread carefully with the chief's wife; there was much at stake. Since the visit wasn't progressing to her satisfaction, she suddenly remembered the basket she was making to trap fish. She had best hurry home and finish it.

Curtailing her call, she excused herself to the unfinished project.

Keeta left puzzled. Why wasn't Essence jealous of Lithia? Nothing Keeta had said ruffled Essence's tranquillity. Here was a woman who refused to be daunted by rumors or facts. Keeta didn't think she liked the chieftain's new squaw.

Chapter Fourteen

The Old Doctor's Fears

The witch doctor clutched wildly at his head. No one must learn of his deteriorating condition or the fears that raged in his confused mind. His longtime diet of fog, smoke, and fermented brew called for a reckoning. Suddenly, he felt powerless as life rushed on, leaving him bobbing in its wake, mouthing old phrases.

It was his job to officiate at the annual induction of braves. The date approached for the ceremony, but he didn't feel like emerging from his tent. *If I can concoct some logical excuse to postpone the event,* he told himself, *I will feel better in a few days.* The chief wouldn't proceed with the meeting against his advice, and he need not know that the old man was merely stalling for time until his health improved.

This was to be an important affair. Keeta's papoose had grown into a strapping lad, straight as a mountain aspen and solid as a quartz stone. The chief had set his heart on the lad; he might even adopt him as his own son and prepare him for the chieftainship.

Such a serious event had never been postponed. The delay might fret the chief, but he feared the witch doctor. Or better said, he feared the gods, and the witch doctor always had his way when he brought the gods into play. And that's what the old man planned to do now.

After the strain of concentration to form his sketchy plan, the doctor sent word to the chieftain that the spirits had appeared to him and bade him wait until a later time for the tribal rites of receiving braves into manhood. The new date was unspecified. Thankfully, the chief never doubted or questioned the diviner's trumped up spirit sessions. (He hadn't before, at any rate.)

The old doctor lay his throbbing head on his pallet, his arms limp. Whatever he did, he must not let the tribe see his humanity. The tribesmen considered him infinite, daring not believe that his life could end. He had held himself before them as an immortal being with supernatural powers, set apart from pain, old age, and death. They must not discover that his leathery old skin would tear when snagged and then fail to heal itself—or that his teeth were rotting out of his pitch-blackened skull and that his bones were brittle.

He had hidden his scarecrow frame beneath many layers of clothing so that no one could see that it was withered like an old tree. The pact he'd made with Mamu many years ago kept his secrets and hers. Each had lived a life of hypocrisy. Now she was dead, thanks be, and had taken some frightful knowledge about the doctor with her. Her death, though a relief to him, whispered to him loudly of his own mortality.

No one knew the dark vices of the witch doctor or his ignoble history. He had not obtained his position honorably. Even now he could hear his mother nagging him to build a fire or bring up water from the spring. She barked that he was the laziest human she'd ever seen. By the time he reached adolescence, she had given up on him entirely. His name—Mogasi—roughly meaning "two faces," matched his melancholy temperament. He was brooding, moody, mean, and slothful.

"You refuse to gather wood!" his mother bellowed. "You cannot ride a mule without clumsily falling off. To shoot a straight arrow is not in you. I will not abide a worthless son. If you can do nothing else, then become a witch doctor like your despicable uncle!"

This idea pleased Mogasi, who had always listed toward his peculiar old uncle whom he called Witch-Witch. He spent hours idling in the tent of Witch-Witch and knew all the ugly masks by name. He feared none of them; respect for the gods was not in the woof of his weave.

"But I don't know how to talk with the spirits!" Mogasi retorted.

"Listen, you dolt: our people are superstitious. They will believe anything you tell them about ghosts and gods. *Pretend* that you are conferring with spirits. Make them think you have no weakness. A man with no weakness is a frightening man. Whether your power is real or not makes no difference. What appears to be real *is* real."

Mogasi launched his career by bullying boys younger and smaller than himself. When he saw how easily it worked, he was most pleased with the results and began to train himself in earnest to be a witch doctor. With the encouragement of his mother, who only wished to have him from under her feet, he decided to take his uncle's place as the tribal medium.

When Mogasi was "ready" for the job, Witch-Witch mysteriously disappeared and was never found. Mogasi took his place quickly—as if it was the normal chain of command—and nobody questioned the transition. He dropped the name his mother had given him and established himself as a mediator between man and the gods. This transpired long before the present chieftain was born, transcending most of the tribe's memory.

Mogasi made a habit of raiding canoes of the white men coming down the river, confiscating their "crazy water." Soon he had become dependent upon the drink.

He had been successful in hiding his past and his frailties from everyone except himself. Now he knew that his aging mind was failing. The old dreams in his old head were all raveled and twisted. His thought escaped like water from broken pottery. Ah, that's what he was: *broken pottery.*

The young chief had a law that frightened the doctor: the death sentence for those not perfect. Did that mandate include old and feeble witch doctors? Lately, Mogasi had to chase off haunting ghosts from his own tent after hearing the wails of empty-armed squaws.

Mamu told him about a child who was born with no hand. Lithia's child. Strangely, he couldn't remember anything in connection with that particular act of destruction. That, of course, didn't mean that it didn't take place. It might only mean that his own memory was at fault. He had said nothing about it lest the chieftain suspect his incompetence. A tremor ran through his bowels and out to his extremities; bones as dry as his would be a bonfire's favorite kindling.

The witch doctor had learned to brew his own "happy juice" from fermented bread and berries. Not for anything must the chief learn of his addiction! The drink helped to drown his fears and kindle a fire in his chest. Over the years, it had been easy to convince the chief that the red glaze in his eyes, his staggery steps, and his slurred speech followed a séance with the spirits.

Mogasi cast his watery eyes about the ragged tent, noticing for the first time that it was as decrepit as himself. He'd repair it when he felt better. The drafts and leaks could give him an ague; his body was perpetually cold as it was. Had the dying already begun? He would fight it! That had always been his way: to resist, resist, resist!

What would happen if he went to sleep and never awoke? The masks about the wall leered at him in mockery. Half sitting up, half falling down, he turned his raddled, skin-folded face away. A gnarl came from the sunken depths of his soul, and the harsh sound hurt as if his throat had been scraped by a dull knife. Who would chase the evil spirits away from him?

Thinking him timeless, the chief had made no provisions for a successor. It would make no difference whether the tribe had a witch doctor or whether they didn't, but the chief did not realize this. The old man grimaced in the gathering darkness, lacking the energy to light a candle. Had those idiotic masks any power to roll back the years and restore his youth and vitality? Had they any power to do *anything?* Of course not!

He had deceived the tribe all this time. In his prime, he felt invincible. But look at him now! He was as old as a leaf in winter. He couldn't arise to chase a field mouse or a beetle from his seedy tent. In truth, he was so blind that he couldn't even see the pesky insects that came to crawl on his decaying body! But worst of all, he hadn't been able to make his "happy water" for three days. Without it, he would surely die!

Outside, the wind whistled and whined, screaming around his tent. It was an eerie, forlorn sound. Monstrous, strangling echoes wormed in from every direction, confusing and meaningless. The world about him blended together, distant, filmy, without voices. He hugged his knees, enclosing the inner storm. He hoped that no emergency called him out during the night; he knew that he would never make it past the tent flap to the region beyond. *Maybe never again.*

The feeling was there like a bitter aftertaste—he couldn't shake it.

Chapter Fifteen

The Eleventh Summer

Five autumns.
Five winters.
Five springs.
Five summers. . . .

It seemed but a few days since she had told the awful lie to spare Broken Bow's life. Now Lithia stared across the landscape, seeing nothing. It was the eleventh summer of her son's life, and time was running out. She had lost her gamble.

The incident in the woods when Broken Bow went for berries verified Lithia's suspicion that the chieftain doubted her story. Each time he rode by their pueblo on his stallion, he glowered. The look gave her jitters.

No superior tribe had conquered the Kotopaxis. Alas, in the entire land, there was no superior tribe. No hunting accident or skirmish with the white man had taken the chief's life. He was stronger and healthier than ever—and his policies were still unreasonable and

103

intense. His single ambition was to have only the best.

A hunt ago, one of his braves was thrown from a horse and crippled. He did not heal, neither did he die from his injuries. Squaw Willow's supplication for the life of her husband brought bitter tears to grease her face, but to no avail. No man would be a liability to the tribe the chieftain said. With ample time to recover, he hadn't. Therefore, he must be eliminated.

For days, when Lithia went to the brook for water, she could hear Willow's wailing. She wanted to stop her ears and run; a knot swelled in her throat where fears broke in, and a voice reminded: *Soon it will be your son.*

When Broken Bow asked why Willow cried, Lithia changed the subject. Broken Bow must not know that he, too, was headed for a dreadful end on his twelfth birthday. How resentful Willow would be if she knew Lithia told the chief a lie to buy time for her child. It hadn't been fair. It hadn't been right. Others suffered. Why not she?

Feeling the squeeze of time, Lithia began a frantic chain of prayer to every god known to her. If they could but forgive her transgression!

She sinned to save her only child; Victor was gone, and her son was all she had. Couldn't they understand that? She petitioned the gods of wind and rain, thunder and lightning and the gods of the seasons. She implored help from the river gods and the mountain gods. She even prayed to the god of death. What had she to lose?

Had she missed any gods? Her whole body was torn with the struggle to get an answer; she listened carefully for a reply. Once when she called to Broken Bow, she heard her own echo and in her extravagant imagination thought it was a god trying to speak to her. But when she grew quiet, the sound ceased. She punished herself to attract the attention of the gods, kneeling on broken pottery and going without nourishment. Yet none responded. Were they all deaf?

Then she began to question their existence. What if they were merely myths? What if there were no gods? When had any of them ever helped anyone? A totem pole made by man could have no more power than the man who fashioned it. Was not the same material used for firewood? What difference could a bit of carving with a knife make? A bone blade could not transform wood into a god! The bolt of revelation overwhelmed her, and she felt near the root of some central issue. If there were no gods at all, then that accounted for their absence of feeling, their lack of compassion. Wood didn't care! Stone couldn't feel or respond!

A tribal atheist! Lithia scolded herself, but could not stop the deliberation. If the chieftain knew of the thoughts that churned in her head, she would be in grave danger of her life. The chief devoutly believed in the gods of the totem pole. *How could he? How could anyone?*

Broken Bow's body was taking on its final shape, his mind adding higher dimensions. He had set the boy without a hand to one side. That one-handed fellow wore his body, but he strode apart in his mind with two good hands that could perform as well as any other young man his age. He asked Lithia's permission to join in the tribal games with his contemporaries. "I can play tag with the buffalo tail as well as the others," he insisted. "It only takes one hand to swat an opponent."

"Oh, no! I would not wish your . . . your missing hand to be laid on the tongues of the . . . the other boys."

"I could hide it beneath my shirt."

"It would not be wise, my son. I cannot let you go."

Confined to the pueblo, the boy yearned for the outdoors; he grew restless and agitated. His childhood timidity was wearing away, and the new boldness worried Lithia more than the passiveness had.

Even if she allowed him the freedoms he wanted in the chief's absence, who was to say the chief wouldn't return unexpectedly and in a foul mood vent his anger on Broken Bow? Or what if an older and stouter boy should injure her son? A second handicap would certainly convince the chief of the gods' curses, and the lie would be exposed. No, Broken Bow must not enlarge his surroundings to include the outdoors.

Her heart ached as Broken Bow stood in the doorway and watched the tribal youngsters practicing archery, tossing a grass target and shooting arrows into it. "I could toss the grass bundle for them," Broken Bow implored.

Lithia said no.

Slate, Keeta's son, was the highest scorer of the clan. His brawny arms bulged as the bowstring grew taut. Broken Bow watched, holding his breath until it burst from his lungs in a blast. Did he remember that this was the boy who shattered his happiness with the ugly story of the chieftain's rule? Lithia wondered. It had been so long ago. . . .

"Could we make a bow, Mama?" Broken Bow asked her.

"Why, we . . . we could try," she said.

With three strands of twisted sinew, they made a bowstring. Lithia, artist by nature, formed a graceful arrow from a slender shaft of hardwood, pointed at one end and feathered on the other. Someday he could shoot it, she promised weakly, but not yet.

Broken Bow called her to the door. "Look, Mama!" He pointed to the playground where a pair of boys rubbed their foreheads together until one yielded. "It doesn't take hands to play that game. I'd like to try my luck at head pushing."

Lithia turned her back so that he could not see her anguish. "No," she whispered.

Each time she said no, she imagined a wall building between her and her son, closing them into separate worlds. A man now peered through the blur of Broken Bow's immaturity, and Lithia knew that every day until the end would require more pressure on the bits. Sometimes they argued, entangled in a web of trivialities. Their wills clashed.

"How shall I ever become a brave if you won't let me out the door?" he challenged. "I will soon be twelve years old!"

"With your birthday, everything will change." The texture of her voice was a strained thinness compounded of grief, exhaustion and futility.

"Then I may go out?"

"Then you will be—free." The answer satisfied Broken Bow, but Lithia walked around in a tense silence. Not knowing the fate that approached, the boy tried to pinpoint the source of his mother's anxiety. Whatever she happened to be doing, a shadow could fall across her like a cloud crossing the valley on a summer day.

He pried for reasons as his perception grew keener. "Mama, when I ask questions, you don't hear me. It seems that your mind is away on a long trip. Your eyes go away, too. They are sad and muddy. Are you becoming ill again?"

"N-no, Broken Bow."

"Your hands work slower when you weave. And your feet stumble."

"It is nothing, son."

Yet as the days passed in rapid succession, Lithia grew more distracted. She tried to flee from her own thoughts but found she couldn't outrun them. Broken Bow joined her beside the campfire one evening intending to ask more questions. She was cooking a fish chowder for him and for herself. Wisps of blue-gray smoke drifted toward the sky. He noticed that her eyes were swollen and gleaming with tears.

"Why are you crying?" he probed.

"The smoke got in my eyes," she said, looking away.

He waited, and when she retreated into the usual silence, he reprimanded her gently. "Your eyes look deep into nowhere," he ventured. "It is not good. I am almost twelve and I will soon be a man. I must know what is troubling you so that I may help bear the weight of it. It is not fair that my lovely mother should carry the basket of worry alone. Two can lift a thing easier than one. Will you not share the problem with me? Tell me: have we not enough food for the coming winter?"

"It isn't that—" Lithia knew that the day had come for her to tell Broken Bow everything; she could keep her secret from him no longer. "It is a dreadful truth!" she told the boy. She shut her eyes tightly, but two small fierce tears spurted out.

"Nothing can be more dreadful than to see you waste away day by day in mind and body," he replied.

With hiccups of misery, the words tumbled out. "What Keeta's son told you many years ago is true," she said. "The chief destroys every imperfect thing, whether it be person or animal. You were born while he was away on an autumn hunt, and Mamu died before she had a chance to report the missing hand to him. For five years, I hid you. Then Keeta told. . . ."

"Then why am I yet alive?" queried the boy, humping his shoulders.

"I told a lie—a terrible and black lie—to spare your life. I hoped to buy time, and I hoped that time would bring a miracle or . . . or some form of rescue.

"I told the chieftain that the gods had kept your

missing hand in their world until your twelfth birthday. Then, when you were of age to be inducted into the tribe's manhood, I said, the gods would give the hand so that you might save the chieftain's life in a fierce battle that would be waged at that time.

"It has been six years since I told the lie. Six years seemed a long while looking ahead, but looking backward, it is nothing.

"Your twelfth year nears, and we will be destroyed: you and I and everything that belongs to us."

"Wouldn't it have been better, Mama, for you to have let the chieftain take me when I was a newborn?"

"No!" She said it savagely. "You were small and helpless! And I loved you too much! At least we've had twelve years together, and now I can die with you. You will not die alone." Suddenly she put her face in her hands. Her hair parted at the nape of her neck and fell across her shoulders to catch her tears. "But, oh, I can see how selfish I have been!" she sobbed. "*Then* you would have had no knowledge of pain and only *I* would have suffered."

"Sweet mother, do not condemn yourself. You did what was best."

"Best? Yes, for me. But not for you. How could I have known that the fateful day would come? I thought . . . I thought that something would happen to the chieftain or . . . or the gods would intervene." She spread her hands with her palms up. "But the gods are worthless, and time has run out."

Venom flew from Broken Bow's eyes, spraying over the pueblo, burning as it went. He felt a rankling hatred for the chieftain. If only *he* could be destroyed! Yet how could a one-handed boy, cursed by the gods and pitied by his tribesmen, so much as throw a stone to frighten a mighty warrior like the chieftain? A vision of the sun-toasted hulk of a man in the woods flashed through his tortured mind.

"The spirit inside of me has been like the raging of a river," Lithia said. "I would like to march to the throne of time and tell the days to stop! I want to scream out for the hours to cease!"

"We will find a way, Mama," Broken Bow said. He put his good hand on her arm, and Lithia noticed that it shook. "You saved me when I was too young to fend for myself, and now I will save you." If only they could flee! But they would certainly be pursued.

Broken Bow fought against depression but lost the battle. *How helpless is a broken bow, how worthless.* The chief was right; a broken bow could never shoot an arrow or win in wartime. A broken bow must be cast aside. . . .

The chieftain was a very good timekeeper, his memory flawless. He would remember that Broken Bow's twelfth birthday was but a fortnight away.

Chapter Sixteen

No Rain

The chieftain was chafed and irritable. His high cheekbones, his heavy jaw, his thin lips—indeed, all his features—joined in the expression of his displeasure. He paced aimlessly. Beneath his feet the earth was hard, covered with a matting of dry, strawlike grass. Many sunrises and sunsets had come and gone, and no rain had fallen. This morning, a raw, red sun chinned itself on the horizon to proclaim another scorching day.

The Kotopaxi tribe was laid out in a loose rectangle along a valley. In the center stood the chief's own house. To the south, Lithia's pueblo faced the east; Keeta lived at the opposite end of the village. The sons of both, as different as rain and drought, were promised by the gods to be outstanding warriors.

Slate, tall and complete, stood a full two harvests above the other lads his age in physique. He won all the arrow shoots and footraces and rode a horse with distinguished showmanship. He could outpush any opponent with his head and outpunch any rival with his fists. The chieftain watched him with growing admiration. He knew brawn when he saw it.

Since I have no sons of my own, he mused, *I might do well to take him as my prodigy.* Slate: a good, solid name with a rock-hard set of muscles behind it. As soon as the witch doctor set the date, the young man would become a brave. The chieftain fumed. Why had the gods chosen to postpone the ceremony that would honor his favorite candidate? Were they in a melancholy fit about something? It irked him to have his plans thwarted.

The other "warrior" coming of age (the chieftain grimaced) was a one-handed runt a full two harvests behind in development. True, he'd had a spunky father, but no similarity existed between father and son. It would help if he bore a likeness of Victor, but the boy wasn't even a dehydrated version of the brave who saved his life. Essence said he should look *inside* of people, but he'd never been able to see past the outside.

The chieftain's eyebrows bunched like enraged caterpillars facing each other for attack. The decision to let the boy live—that had been six years ago now—was the hardest of the chieftain's life. It went against his grain to bend his law for some supposed vision.

Lithia was a beautiful woman. She had a delicate build that reminded him of a flower on a slender stalk. Maybe his desire for her had misled him. When he had proposed marriage, she had turned him down shamelessly. Then she said she had been commissioned by the gods to devote herself to rearing the blemished child.

Misgivings scratched at the chief's hindsight. Why would the gods need to assign a woman to protect their property? Why couldn't they have cared for the boy themselves if (aha, *if*) they had chosen him as a special ambassador for the tribe?

The boy seldom stepped outside the walls of his pueblo, and when he did, he was mother-shadowed. There again, if the gods had a specific plan for him, he would come to no harm. Lithia's hovering wasn't necessary.

The wisp of a kid could never shoot an arrow; he couldn't ride a horse. His skin was disgracefully blanched for a boy. He had never participated in head butting or footraces. With his antisocial manner, it would take a miracle of transformation for him to become anything even *with* a magic hand.

He had caught the boy in the woods once picking berries: *a woman's job!* When he thought about it, his teeth clamped tight together. He would have ended the boy's life that day had not the gods sent a rabid animal to charge his horse.

What could the gods possibly see in the ruin of humanity? The very thought of the sallow underling galled the chief, but he must take care to hide his vexation from the gods in case this was their special project. Gods could be most fickle and unpredictable.

He walked on beyond the village, taking note of the twigs that broke with a crackle, thirsting for moisture. The river had narrowed to a tiny rope of water; each week it seemed to shrink like a green hide left in the sun. The once lush grass was a sickly yellow. Even now the deadly heat bore down without mercy on the chief's bare shoulders, overbaking them.

The tribe had never experienced such a drought. Every new day dawned with its own disaster. Soon the entire population would languish for lack of drinking water. The horses—and that included his own beloved stallion—were thinning in the flanks for want of fodder. What tribe could hope to win a battle with underfed horses? He kicked at the powder-dry ground, spattering his beaded boot with dust.

The chieftain was spirit-tired. The previous week's hunt had taxed his nerves. Wasted! His time had been utterly wasted! An unproductive venture had a way of trying his patience to the limit. He had found no deer, elk, antelope, or buffalo; the animals had moved to other areas for food and water. He hadn't even seen a lanky rabbit! He'd killed nothing but a white man—and had failed to get his scalp, a disappointment that added to his other grievances.

What he needed was a conference with the witch doctor. Anything to bring rain! And quickly! Something was amiss, and he must have some answers. He turned back toward the village, running now, brushing dirt and sweat from his face. Yes, he had to see that mediator at once.

The senile doctor sat in his shabby tent, shaking his head from side to side, chanting senseless monosyllables. Only a small piece of his mind was left.

The chieftain was no stranger to the seer's tent; he'd been there many times before. He didn't like the shadows and sickening herb smells or the uneasy rustlings. (He didn't know that the rustlings were rats.) But he endured these things, telling himself that the end justified the means.

The hideous masks stacked against the wall intimidated the chief. He was careful to keep his distance from their grotesque sneers. They had to be ugly, of course, to frighten away the bodiless heads that caused sickness. The witch doctor had explained it like this: "As the powerful is overcome by the more powerful, even so the ugly is chased away by the more ugly." This, he said, was a great proverb of unfathomable wisdom.

Claw hooks held bones, teeth, and the awesome medicine pipe. But most precious of all was the sacred bundle from which the chieftain kept a respectable distance. No one knew what the bundle contained, and no one dared ask. It had existed from the beginning of time, and the loss of it would be the worst possible tribal disaster. The doctor guarded it with his life . . . not that anyone would touch it!

In response to the chieftain's voice, the doctor bowed low in homage. "What may I do for you, my most esteemed chief?" he asked. "At your disposal is seven thousand years of life contained in this dark and fleshless form." It was a phrase he'd memorized. When he'd given the obeisance, he found it hard to straighten himself up again.

"We have a serious problem, O revered one." The chief spoke with a clipped tone.

"Eh? And what might that be?" The aged witch doctor was unaware that a drought persisted. It had been many days since he had groped from his dilapidated tent.

The stench and heat of the room made the chief gasp for air. He clenched his nostrils to shut out the moldy smell, a conglomerate of dankness and spoilage and other details of human filth he determined not to think about. "Many sunrises and sunsets have come and gone, and no rain has fallen to bless our grasslands," the chief explained. "Our horses are weakening; our river is as narrow as a needle. The wild animals we depend on for food have moved away. The hunt went badly again today."

"Eh? Oh . . ." The old doctor groaned piteously, whether from aching joints or the bad news an observer would not know. "The . . . the gods. Yes, I shall consult . . ." his low, banal voice died away. He pounded his head to force it to cooperate. Oh, yes . . . it was his duty to encourage the good spirits and subdue the evil ones. The vigor with which he once performed the rites was gone; he lacked the energy for a melodramatic dispatch.

Aware that the chief was watching and expecting a solution, he brought his arthritic hands up to his bony cheeks in a shocked gesture. Then trying to sort sounds and sights that had become confused in the mad throbbing of his brain, he shrieked, "Some member of the tribe has displeased the gods!" His shrill voice turned to a lamentation. "You must hold a rain dance in the darkest part of the night: between moondown and sunup. Here! Take my sacred drum, for it is round like the heavens and the earth, and it carries in it the sacred powers of both.

"Summon sixteen of your most gallant warriors and let them dance four at a time." He held up his sticklike fingers. "Only those who have taken scalps of an enemy are worthy." He hesitated as if listening for further instructions from an unseen specter. "Each warrior is to bring his own whistle, rattle, or flute to awaken the sleeping gods.

"Obey my words with utmost diligence, for the gods must be brought from their slumber in a responsive mood or all is useless. If you thus beseech the gods, we will know by this time tomorrow why we have been cursed. Go! I shall chant to the gods all night!"

It had been a long, laborious dialogue for the aged man, and his breath came in short, hard blasts. The chief bowed himself to the floor in a gesture of submission and slipped hurriedly from the tent.

The witch doctor's shrunken face contorted with an evil smile. He had fooled the chieftain again! The palsied remnant of a man folded his fragile body onto the malodorous sheepskin and closed his papery eyelids.

Chapter Seventeen

Refuge

The day took on the proportions of a nightmare. Lithia's face felt stiff and raw from weeping. She sat numbly, knowing that all hope was aborted and wondering if there was some way she could prepare herself for tomorrow. She had expended the luxury of the lie she told six years ago.

Tomorrow was Broken Bow's twelfth birthday, and she would witness his death while her heart died within her. Then she and all her belongings would be burned to ashes.

It was blasphemy to tell an untruth on the gods. She knew it, but she had been brazen enough to take the risk for her son. Now she found herself confused and lost in a labyrinth of half-formed thoughts: Was it worth . . . ? What else . . . ? How could . . . ? Scalding tears blazed a trail down her cheeks and anguish cramped her stomach.

Broken Bow sat against the wall, riddled with fear and anger. He had refused the fry bread she offered, his untouched bowl collecting summer flies. He sat immobile, and when she reached out to comfort him, he turned away. He had climbed down inside himself and shut the door. Lithia never knew his stillness could be so terrible or cut her heart so deeply. She remembered what Victor had once said: *For small griefs you cry aloud, but big griefs are borne within.*

For one brief moment, she scanned the horizon of memory for Victor. It had been so long, she'd lost the picture of his face, the sound of his voice. "Victor, I didn't know what else to do for our papoose." She was talking to a stranger.

"Oh, Broken Bow, I am sorry!" she moaned. "To all the gods I apologize. I beg forgiveness!" The stress of the years piled on her, threatening to rob her of her sanity. She thrust her fist into her mouth, biting down on her knuckles to stop her crying.

There was so much she wanted to do, to say on this last day. But words would not come to tell of love or hate or death. There was nothing to do but wait, wait. . . . And it seemed that the waiting would strain her heart to breaking.

The door stood open, and through it hurled a flying form. Lithia jumped and Broken Bow sank his head into the darkness of his cupped hands. Was this a vision? Or had the chieftain sent someone with the speed of light to snatch Broken Bow for the death ceremony a day early?

Grabbing for a blanket to cover himself, the rolling figure came to rest near Broken Bow. There the hump lay motionless, proof that it had come to a standstill. Not a noise did the apparition make.

Fearing everything and expecting anything, Lithia hoped this might be an embodied god who had come to bless—or perhaps curse—their pitiful existence. She cared not who or what the thing was as long as it wasn't the chief's death messenger. Death at the hands of the gods might be more humane than the chief's method.

Still the wraith lay fixed. Had they really seen anything at all, or had a gust of wind blown the blanket into a heap beside Broken Bow? Lithia stared, unwilling to turn her head, but Broken Bow was too frightened to open his eyes.

If this was a god, Lithia didn't want to frighten him by a disruptive move, especially if he had come to help them. Happiness, she'd learned, was like a brittle shell: motion or noise could shatter it.

But if it should be an envoy from the chief, they couldn't hope to escape anyhow; they were helplessly trapped in the pueblo with an unknown mound under the cover.

Beneath the sheath, Peregrine Abelard peeled back the layers of time and relived the last momentous hours of his life. He had gone into the woods to pray, seeking a place apart to talk to his God. Discouragement plagued his soul while the yeast of frustration worked in his mind. He had gained such few souls for Christ! His efforts on this new continent were so futile. Was it worth leaving a widowed mother back in the old country to come to a strange land and see no results? Where had he failed?

He had never doubted his missionary call to the Indian tribes, but how superstitious they were! They worshiped gods of every sort, tortured by these nonexistent masters. Had not he come upon a bevy of these gods carved into the wood of a totem pole that rested deep in the woods? Had it not seemed that the evil spirits were challenging his right to invade their territory? He had cast the idol into the fast-moving river, realizing all the while that the destroying of a single idol wouldn't make a dent in the idolatry of these savages.

As much a part of God's creation as the white man, these primitive people were afraid of owls, echoes, and even the white man himself. Alas, they believed that their own shadows were spirits following them about!

How could he teach a nation that was afraid of his pale face? And those vile witch doctors! They held uncanny powers over both mind and body, and only God Himself could break their influence. Peregrine felt crushed beneath his heavy burden.

Along the coastline, the friendly tribes had been dishearteningly unresponsive, but one would be flirting with eternity to approach a hostile tribe without an injunction direct from heaven. A white man was a ready target, a detested object to the uncivilized tribes inland. And what man wanted his toenails boiled and made into glue?

Yet Peregrine Abelard felt a deep call of God to a rebel tribe somewhere. The gnawing inside had driven him into the woods to be alone with his Maker today. What turmoil thrashed about in his soul as he grappled for answers! He must have walked deeper into the brush than he had intended, for before he could climb a tree or dart into the underbrush, he was surrounded by the brilliantly painted bodies of Indian warriors.

Peregrine Abelard was weaponless. That is, unless his New Testament, a pocketknife, one lone coin, and his faith in God could be considered artillery. At that moment, he did as he had done many times before: he committed himself to God's care and protection.

Would the Reverend Abelard's faith have been overcharged had he known that he was up against an undefeated chief who destroyed all cripples and who boasted twenty enemy scalps—or that the pole the parson had cast into the river belonged to this very tribe? Probably not. The chieftain's many scars, relics of tortures he'd suffered to honor his gods, told the perceptive missionary that this was no ordinary brave; this was the leader of a special tribe.

An arrow from the chief's bow hissed toward Peregrine, striking the hand he'd thrown up to defend himself. As the thud of the flint echoed back to his pursuer, Peregrine rolled under a low shrub and disappeared. He thanked God for his right hand. It had saved him.

The chief found his arrow, identified with his Kotopaxi markings. But why was the arrow not swathed in blood? It sounded as if the arrow had hit a tree, but he had seen it hit the white man. Somewhere the enemy lay dead. Puzzled, the chief followed the bloodless trail, assured that his victim's body bloated nearby. He searched the woods long and diligently. He'd never seen a scalp like that one, and he wanted it to add to his collection.

Instead, God's man zigzagged through the tangling resistance of woods and plunged into an opening cleared by the village. He sped through the door of Lithia's pueblo; it was the nearest place of safety.

From the markings he saw as he raced in, Peregrine decided this was probably the famous Kotopaxi tribe that he had heard about, the one he'd mentioned to his mother in a recent letter. He had shallowly studied their language and symbols, doubtful that he'd ever find an opportunity to preach the gospel to this notorious tribe; no missionary had ever lived to do so.

Their chief, a fearsome giant with black eyes and blue-black hair (the man who had taken a shot at him), collected white scalps like trinkets on a string. He had killed his own father whose only felony was old age. After catching a glimpse of the chief, Peregrine decided that all he'd heard was believable. He had often included this tribe in his prayers, but his mind could not contrive a way for them to hear the salvation story.

As Peregrine sat hunched beneath an Indian woman's blanket, he thanked God again and again for sparing his life. Oh, yes, he was willing to face death for the gospel. But how could a corpse bring the good news to people steeped in darkness? What would happen from this point, he didn't know. That was not his problem; it was God's—and he felt God's mighty hand upon him right now. His faith took wings, and he suppressed an urge to shout "Hallelujah!" aloud, restraining himself for fear the outburst would further startle his hostess.

Hadn't God sent him here? He had been praying when he was cast slapdash through this very doorway. Was this God's unorthodox means of getting him into the tribe to preach? Peregrine's heart gave a joyful leap at the thought. If he could impart his message, then he would be willing to die.

After a while, Peregrine pushed the blanket to one side and sat up. His eyes moved about the sod walls, touching each object softly. Then they fell upon a mournful mother and a boy. Both were frozen with fear.

Chapter Eighteen

The Letter

Back in the old country, Marie Abelard eased the amber pastry from the oven with her pot mitten and set the teapot to boil. The aroma of sweetbread filled the house from gable to cellar, colliding with the darkness that crept into the edges of the kitchen. In bygone days, she had sold pastries in the duchy. The small salary enabled her, by economy and self-denial, to educate her two sons.

As Marie lit the lamp that stood on the sideboard, her hand brushed against the silver notes of the dinner gong that hung on the wall. She would eat her bread alone tonight unless a guest from the hamlet happened by for a friendly visit. The dinner gong had been silent for months now.

Early that morning, she had made a gingerbread dough with thick sour milk, including the faithful cow in her offering of thanks. Pulling out the bread riser with the squeaky handle, she set the bread. This ritual stemmed from her young bride days, but she still followed it religiously once a week "just in case" the boys came home or a footsore traveler needed a meal. It didn't seem that life was on the right tack until she had started her bread.

She hummed a bit of a tune. Out of habit, her hand reached up to tame her cloud of soft, blowy hair now the color of autumn sedge. This was a day the Lord had made; she would rejoice and be glad in it. It had been a good day, but it closed like the storekeeper's shutters at night with no word from the boys. She glanced out the window once more in hopeful anticipation as the sunlight's last shimmer faded over the glen.

A spotless linen cloth covered the table, and in the center sat her favorite vase. How she treasured that vase! In the spring it spilled over with wildflowers from the meadow below. Her own Lewis had carved it for her. Lewis, the older of her boys, seemed to be born with the knack for making wooden carvings come alive. The figures he hewed and shaped looked real.

How could brothers be so different? They were as opposite as any two children a mother could have netted at random from the ocean of life. Lewis, the talented one, lacked the serious nature of his brother, Peregrine. Peregrine's feelings ran deep; he had been sensitive to God even as a youngster. She had found him poring over the family Bible when he was scarcely out of bibs. If she was unable to attend church, he would go to the vine-clad sanctuary alone. Not Lewis! He used every excuse to stay home from church to play or whittle. It wasn't that Lewis was a bad boy; he just wasn't spiritually oriented like his brother.

Hence it did not come as a surprise to Marie when her younger son, Peregrine—still on the tender side of twenty—told her of his missionary call to the New

World and its natives. It was a much greater surprise when the elder, Lewis, declared that he would go along to "seek his fortune" in the New World and keep a protective eye on young Peregrine.

Since the accident, Lewis seemed to feel a responsibility to his brother. Lewis and Peregrine had been chopping wood when Lewis's axe slipped from his grip and severed Peregrine's hand from his arm. Lewis blamed himself for sharpening the axe to such a cutting edge, for his carelessness, and for not doing the work by himself. After all, he was five years older, larger and stronger than his sibling.

It seemed to Marie that Peregrine had suffered more than his share of peril since birth; his guardian angel was obliged to work overtime to keep him in the land of the living. Was the enemy trying to destroy him to keep him from his future mission?

It had been more than a year since the boys had gone to America. Webbed memories drifted in and out, like shadows, leaving a lonely ache. On the one hand, she wanted to hold her sons to herself, and on the other, she wanted to give them to the Lord. Sometimes she was sure the mixed emotions would rupture her heart. It was so far across the waters, and word came so seldom.

Would she ever see her children again? Surely she must learn to trust more. But what earthly mother could read of scalpings and massacres without qualms? When fear seized her, she cast herself to her knees beside her bed where a faded throw rug became her altar until peace came. She called this "stuffing her cares in the knothole of faith."

Marie could never doubt Peregrine's call; her mother heart sensed his burden before he spoke of it. Had he gone alone, she could not have borne the anxiety. Lewis went for adventure and the lure of fortune, but he would be his brother's keeper, too. The fact that her sons were together gave Marie a consolation in spite of her emptiness. Lewis did not understand Peregrine's spiritual nature and had poked harmless fun at him over the years, but beneath his good-humored banter, he loved and respected his little brother and would defend him against the world. Woe be unto anyone else who ridiculed him!

Dusk came and Marie picked up her Bible for her evening devotion. The verse that opened to her was Isaiah's writing: "Thou wilt keep him in perfect peace, whose mind is stayed on thee: because he trusteth in thee." She began to hum again and was startled by a sharp rap on her front door.

Marie swung the door open wide to welcome the delivery boy from the hamlet, glad to have one with whom to share her pastry. Nobody loved her gingerbread, coated with its sugary film, better than Carrel.

"The ship came in from the New World today," he announced as she sliced him a generous portion of the bread and poured his cup of tea.

The teapot stopped, suspended in midair. "Any news from my wanderers?" she asked quickly, and just as quickly, Carrel produced her letter.

She reached for it with eager hands. "Please do excuse me, Carrel, while I read my letter, for I cannot possibly wait." She sat down and read it in a gobble, her hungry eyes trying to take in the whole page at once. Peregrine had written for both himself and Lewis:

Mother dear,

We are well. Lewis found a job to his liking, carving furnishings for the wealthy. He is being paid well.

My own report is meager. My burden grows heavier each day. I have accomplished nothing for my Master. My spirit tells me that God's purpose will be fulfilled soon, but I am blinded by human doubts. I plead with you to bear me up in prayer, my dear mother. I am willing to give my life to take the gospel to the natives of this new country.

A strong and savage tribe lies to the west. I have an uncommon interest in the tribe. Their chief is a powerful man who worships idol gods of all sorts. He kills anyone in his tribe who is crippled or imperfect. Perhaps it is because I was injured in the woodcutting accident that I cannot bear to think of such cruelty. Yet I cannot conceive of a way to reach them. God is working, but oh, that I might understand what He is doing!

I miss the sweetmeats and butter. Life is not easy for me here, but neither was it easy for my Lord. I count myself unworthy to suffer for Him.

Now I must tell you about the idol god that I found in the woods. While walking in the forest, seeking direction from my Counselor, I came upon a small opening in the bushes. Lying there with shavings from recent carving was a perfectly formed totem pole with the most gruesome of faces. The sculpturing was quite as good as Lewis's.

I felt as if the demons were peering at me from those faces, claiming their territory. The idol was complete (or almost so) and I suppose that it belonged to the tribe I mentioned earlier, though I have no way of knowing for sure. The eyes of the gods seemed to challenge my right to be here in the new land. I hope that the tribe to whom it belongs has made room for "the unknown God" as Paul's acquaintances at Mars Hill did; I would like to be the one to introduce them to Him.

As my God would wish, I removed the idol even as the prophets of old removed the Israelites' gods from the groves. It was no easy task to drag the evil-looking thing through the underbrush to the swiftly flowing river. I was out of strength when I got to the water and cast the icon face down to be carried away to the sea. But the overflowing power of God refreshed me, and even as I cast it away, I felt victory!

> *Your prayers sustain me. I remain your faithful son,*
> *Peregrine*

It was a long letter for Peregrine, and Marie hugged it to her breast, already craving the rereading. She thanked Carrel for bringing the message so late in the day. Then she sent him on his way with a loaf of fresh bread for his mother.

As she knelt to pray over the letter, she was mercifully unaware that her son, Peregrine, was in the midst of the greatest danger of his life.

Chapter Nineteen

The Apparition

Broken Bow turned his eyes slowly and fearfully toward the image that sat in the floor of the pueblo. The form was a small white man scarcely larger than himself. His eyes were a peculiar shade of sky color and his hair the hue of buttercups. The white man was smiling!

Broken Bow found his tongue first. "Is . . . is it a w-white man or is it a g-god, Mama?" he stuttered.

At no other time would Lithia have protected a white man. Had not a white man's fire machine killed her beloved Victor? Had not she vowed wrath upon any white devil who crossed her path in life? Besides, the chieftain would add to her grim sentence if she concealed an enemy. (Alas, if a greater punishment was possible!)

But hark! Would not this be the best possible way to get even with the arrogant chieftain? To be a traitor—to betray him flagrantly—on the eve of her son's destiny?

Oh, she could have loved that handsome man at one

129

time with as great an intensity as she now hated him except for his inane ruling that caught her son in its whiplash. But how fine a line between love and hate! Today she loathed the chieftain with a malice that superseded her hatred for the white man. Ah, sweet vengeance! She might as well rile the chief to the hilt while she was at it. She had nothing to lose, because tomorrow . . .

Peregrine Abelard looked about the pueblo, still smiling broadly. He studied the bone combs, stone scrapes, and gourd dishes. They were of simple design and might have belonged to any clan. Then he saw the baskets: they had their own unique weave that identified the tribe. *The mighty Kotopaxis.* His lips moved in a petition for wisdom. This was the chance he'd been praying for! Carefully must he follow the Holy Spirit's direction.

To Lithia's surprise, the white stranger spoke a few words in her language. With gestures and signs, he explained as best he could that he had been pursued by the chieftain and had sought refuge in her pueblo, nearest the wood's edge. The chief, supposing him dead, was likely still searching for his body. Peregrine made a running motion with the fingers of his left hand and pointed to himself. He had escaped the chieftain. Then he laughed; to him there was nothing funnier than a calamity that didn't quite happen.

Lithia found gladness in her heart that this small white man had eluded the chieftain. She had never agreed with the custom of scalping. Indeed, she had never understood the concept of one human hurting another.

The stranger's voice, gentle and kind, intrigued Broken Bow. His terror dissolved. It was the boy's first sighting of a white man, and he gaped at the man's well-trimmed beard, his tailored pantaloons, and his buckled shoes. A smile picked at his lips.

Broken Bow's curiosity didn't bother Peregrine. He

liked children and understood their inquisitiveness. But Lithia's expression did bother him. He made her to know that he would leave their pueblo as soon as night came to cover his movements. Certainly he would not wish to jeopardize their lives by his presence here. He groped for words, asking God to help him enlighten their souls in the short time he would be with them.

"What is your name?" he asked Lithia.

"Lithia," she said. "It means a stone."

"You have no—brave?"

"He is dead."

"I am sorry." He traced a line down his face with a finger to indicate a trail of tears.

"It was long ago. I have forgotten."

"And what can I offer you for saving my life today?" Lithia shook her head. "Nothing."

"White man's money?" Peregrine held out his lone coin. He had planned to buy bread with it, but God would supply his needs. Hadn't God fed Elijah with birds for couriers?

The coin fascinated the boy, but Lithia again shook her head.

Peregrine offered his small New Testament. "Book?" The Indian woman would not be able to read the Bible, and Peregrine did hate to part with it since it had been a gift from his dear old grandmother, but sometimes the fancy of these natives called for unusual objects. Besides, God might have a plan for leaving His Word behind in this camp.

Broken Bow's eyes glistened, but Lithia's eyes narrowed with decision. "No."

Peregrine removed the knife from his pocket; he had little use for it and Indians loved trinkets. Surely this would be the thing Lithia would choose as compensation for her kindness.

"White man's knife?"

Broken Bow leaned forward and brought one hand from behind his back. What a prize the knife would be! No other young man in the Kotopaxi tribe had such a trophy.

"No!" Lithia said it sharply.

"What then?" Peregrine spread his hands flat in a questioning gesture. Sure that this pretty squaw risked severe punishment for shielding him, he felt the weight of his debt. He had nothing more to offer. "Is there anything I can do?"

"We want nothing!" The words poured out like a cloudburst. "For tomorrow we die!"

"Because of me?" Peregrine pressed. He could not bear the thought that the squaw's conscience would nag her to confess his presence in her pueblo, bringing death upon her family. What irreparable damage had he done by coming to her dwelling? How could any good come of such a blunder? An act so imprudent on his part could not possibly tie in with God's plan for saving the tribe. He berated himself without lenience, billing the price of their lives to his own account.

"You will die because I came to your home?" he asked again, pointing to himself to make his question clear. "I will be the cause of your death?"

"No."

"But why? Can I help to save you as you have saved me?"

"No one can save us!" The bitterness spilled out. "The chieftain hates my son." Helplessness, anxiety, and a plea for deliverance: all these emotions camped in the eyes of the desperate mother. "He has no hand. Show him, Broken Bow."

Broken Bow pulled his right arm from behind his back. "See," Lithia pointed. "He is not a strong bow to hunt, to fight, to ride swift horses. My son was cursed by the gods at birth." The gall of her words stained her voice. "The chief kills broken bows."

"Tell me more," gestured Peregrine. "Please tell me more."

"I do not know why my baby was cursed at birth!" exploded Lithia. "He had a noble father who gave his life for the chieftain!"

Peregrine waited.

"I told a lie to the chieftain in order to spare my child's life. I loved my son so! I could not bear to see him killed!"

"What did you tell the chief?"

"I told him that the gods had kept the hand in a golden box and that when my son was twelve years old he would be blessed with a magic hand to help the chief in battle. It was an untruth. No gods will come to give my son a new hand. We are doomed!

"There is only one night between us and death. Tomorrow is my son's twelfth birthday—" Having exposed her bleeding heart, Lithia gave way to waves of weeping. Her misery enveloped the room.

Peregrine's soul was stirred with compassion and pity. If only they knew his God! His lips parted in unspoken prayer.

Then he sensed that God was laying the cornerstone upon which to build His miracle. With the confidence of Peter and John when they met the lame man at the Gate Beautiful, Peregrine Abelard said: "Perhaps *I* cannot help, but I know Someone who can save you and your Broken Bow from death."

Chapter Twenty

The God of Love

Struggling to hurdle the language barriers, Peregrine tried diligently to introduce Lithia to God. It was his greatest challenge: to describe a big, good God with few and small words. Oh, for a broader vocabulary!

"I do not understand," repeated Lithia over and over, but Broken Bow listened intently, and it seemed to Peregrine that the frail youth comprehended more with his keen mind than did his groping mother. The boy would often interpret wisps of conversation for her.

Insight came slowly, but the bits that Lithia grasped filled her with awe. This white man knew a Jesus God made of love: nothing but love. The joy of knowing such a God beamed from his face and infected her.

Lithia's gods were made of wood and stone, sinister in design and as lifeless as the material from which they were hewn; they were no gods at all. The Jesus God was a sovereign, living God who made the wood and stone in the beginning.

This God, Peregrine said, loved everybody and everything. He didn't curse innocent babies who were born less fortunate than others. This God loved broken bows, blinded eyes and crippled feet. He loved the old and the infirm. How different He was from the tribal gods who demanded bodily perfection! How eagerly Lithia listened!

The white man said that God loved *her* Broken Bow. Tears rained freely down Lithia's cheeks; no one had ever loved Broken Bow but herself.

Perceiving Lithia's hunger to hear the gospel, Peregrine hurried on. He would not be able to stay long without discovery; Indians were adept at following footprints.

"The God of love came down to our world from His home in heaven," he explained, pointing up. "He came as a baby wrapped in a coat of skin like you and me so that He would know how we feel when we're sick, sad, or angry. He stayed for a few years, and while He was here, He healed many broken bows and sightless arrows. He even put life back into a dead boy for his mother. He could make a new hand if He wished." He held up the Bible. "His story is here."

"I cannot read," Lithia said. "You must tell me."

Peregrine continued, anointed now. "Because He suffered a broken heart Himself, he knows the hurt of your heart. The people hated Jesus, and He was put to death by men as thoughtless as the chieftain—"

"Oh!" moaned Lithia. "Then the God of love is now dead?"

"No! No!" Peregrine patted the Bible. "The story is here."

"I cannot read," repeated Lithia. "You must tell me."

"Death could not hold pure love. After three days," he held up three fingers, "Jesus came out of the grave to live forever. He is alive now. But He gave His life for the Kotopaxi tribe and the whole world."

"If He saw my Broken Bow, He might not—"

"His Spirit is everywhere. He sees your Broken Bow today. He does not see a crippled boy when he looks at your son; God looks on the *inside*. He doesn't care how imperfect the body might be. The outside holds the true man inside."

Am I making Your Word plain enough, God? It would be easier, Peregrine decided, to compile a school primer than to perform the task assigned him. However, he felt God working through him with power and perceived that the emotions of Lithia and the boy were touched. He watched them seesaw between joy and tears. They "ate" faster than he could feed them.

Peregrine went on: "Jesus, the God of love, hears every prayer. His Spirit is near to those who believe in Him. All one has to do is ask for what he needs."

"That is all?" Lithia asked. A smile brightened her eyes, lighting up their darkness.

"He wants us to be like Him," Peregrine said. "We must be filled with love for others, forgiving those who have wronged us."

"Oh, I could never be like Him!" worried Lithia. "My head is filled with bad thoughts! I hate the chieftain because he destroys innocent people."

How could he help her over the unbridgeable chasm of hate? He felt hopelessly unsupplied with words.

"And Keeta!" spat Lithia. "Her tongue has brought me so much trouble that I cannot love her. . . . Oh, what shall I do?"

"You must forgive—"

The padding of feet came, and then they stopped. *Keeta!* She must not see the white man in Lithia's pueblo. Lithia hurled herself toward the door, burying

Peregrine beneath the blanket on her way there.

"Lithia—"

"You must not come in, Keeta." Lithia blocked her entry.

"I want to tell you about the chieftain's new squaw and about the rain dance tonight."

"No, Keeta, I—"

"Essence is truly beautiful, Lithia. She is the perfect squaw for our chieftain. She said he needed her because he made such dreadful johnnycake. She was married before and had two children, but they got swept away in a flood because the gods needed—"

"Really, Keeta, I haven't time to visit just now. I am very busy today."

"I'll come in and talk while you work."

"I don't think you would want to. We have something contagious here."

"Something contagious?"

"Yes, quite. It works on your insides."

"And you haven't called the witch doctor?"

"No—"

"I will get him for you."

"We are much better, Keeta. There is no need."

The heat outside was intense; there was no air to breathe. Keeta panted. "I thought I heard a voice when I came—"

"My son and I were talking."

"There are footprints to your door."

"I went out earlier to fetch water."

Keeta tried to peer beyond Lithia with quick, restless glances. Lithia moved to block her view.

"What is under the blanket?"

"Something that my son and I are working on. There's a knife under there and some silver, but we have not finished with it yet."

"Is it a god you are working on?"

"If you must know, God is working on us!"

"That doesn't make sense, Lithia."

"It makes perfect sense."

"Well, I did want to tell you about the rain dance. The witch doctor told the chief that someone in our tribe has greatly displeased the gods, and the tribe must be purged of the offender before the rain will come."

"We will talk about it later, Keeta. I must see to other needs now. Please excuse me."

Chapter Twenty-One

The Hand

The sky, graying into thick twilight, told Peregrine Abelard that it would soon be time to go. Evening had tacked its four corners down over the horizon. The missionary would have to trust God to complete his unfinished work.

Studying the formation of Broken Bow's right arm, he said, "I have something for your son."

Broken Bow stirred with anticipation. Would it be the knife? Or the black Book about the loving God? Or the shiny coin?

Peregrine pointed to his own right hand, and only then did Lithia notice that it was made of wood. She watched with amazement as he removed it from his body and fastened it to Broken Bow's stub of an arm. Now Broken Bow had two hands like the other boys in the tribe.

"It isn't practical," Peregrine told them. "It won't work; it is wooden. The fingers cannot move. But it looks as natural as life, doesn't it?" Then he explained that he had lost his hand in a wood-chopping accident when he was a lad no older than Broken Bow. His brother, Lewis, had fashioned the prosthesis for him. He said he was sure his brother would carve another for him if Broken Bow would like to keep this one.

Broken Bow heralded his satisfaction with a beaming face, and his acceptance of the hand pleased Peregrine. Each knew the torturous awkwardness of a missing member; they experienced a rapport that Lithia could not share.

"It was the wooden hand that saved my life in the woods today," the missionary told Lithia. "When the chieftain shot the fatal arrow, I threw up my hand and the arrow took the blow." With his finger, Peregrine traced the scar made by the oversized flint. "See where it struck?"

Broken Bow studied the mark raptly. Was not this deep V-shaped indention another proof that the loving God was taking care of the white stranger who believed and trusted in Him? Would not He do the same for an Indian boy?

While Broken Bow's heart gathered the fruit of faith from the missionary's planting, his thoughts raced faster than a roebuck. Could it be that this God sent the angry animal to charge the chieftain's horse that day in the woods so that Broken Bow's life would be spared? Did the loving God care that much for a handless nobody? And might that same God find a way to spare his life on the morrow?

By the dissipating light, Broken Bow inspected the artificial limb. The hand matched his skin tones better than it matched the pale complexion of the white man. Why, it looked as if it belonged on Broken Bow's body! It would pass for a real, live hand.

A joyful thought struck the boy: Maybe—just maybe—the chieftain would see the hand and suppose it to be the magic hand promised by the gods in his mother's story. How could the chief guess that a white fugitive had sought shelter in their pueblo and left such a unique gift in departing? Could this be God's way of answering prayer? He reached for hope with the instinct of a starving child for food.

If Lithia harbored such thoughts, that possibility didn't stay anchored at dock. There would be no deceiving the astute chieftain. A wooden hand would mean nothing more than a log for the fire tomorrow. She had already fooled the chief one time too many; to try to trick him again might bring unthinkable torture.

Only the Jesus God could change the prideful chieftain's heart of stone. Lithia's job was to put away her own hate and bitterness so that her spirit could be right for such a good Deity. And she doubted her ability to do her part.

"It is dark now, and I must go," Peregrine said.

Lithia wanted to ask more questions, but there was not time and only her fear that the man would be found and killed eased the emptiness she felt when she thought of him slipping away into the night, forever exiting her life. She considered the paradox of her situation: despite the peril the man's presence brought to her home, she had never felt safer. Besides, he had brought a crumb of hope to her table of hopelessness.

"God sent me to your pueblo." Peregrine's statement was heavy with conviction. "I shall pray that my God will send a miracle for you tomorrow. I know that help will come from Him." They were his parting words.

Peregrine hurried away, almost colliding with a pair of rushing feet before the dark forest swallowed him.

His mind churned with uncertainties. Was he sent to

America to tell one squaw and her son about the true God? If, indeed, they died on the morrow, they would take the truth with them to their graves and it would spread no farther. Would this be his only opportunity to witness to this tribe? Was he directed to Lithia's house solely to escape death for himself? Or to give his hand to a dismembered child?

Oh, no! The Spirit spoke to Peregrine's heart, and faith arose, drubbing all doubts, whispering that this was only the beginning. Someday he would return to the Kotopaxi tribe.

Chapter Twenty-Two

The Rain Dance

The witch doctor awoke with a start. A ferocious headache painted black and white designs inside his head, a head thrust forward in a position which bespoke of eternal listening. The designs wove themselves into fearsome shapes. His brain filled with a whirring that dislodged his thoughts, shifting them back and forth from childhood to the present so fast that he couldn't be certain where he was in time. What was that noise? Was his mother calling him? Or was it Witch-Witch pointing a condemning finger at him from the grave? The pain drained from his head to his stomach as though he were being poured from one gourd to another. Every part of him shook convulsively. *The noise . . . ?*

Oh, yes. It was the rain dance he'd ordered. Well, he had best do his part. He pushed himself to his knees and lit a candle. Then he felt around for his colored sands. With these he smeared a crude picture on the floor of his tent. As the picture was erased, the figures would carry the prayer for rain to the wife of the wind god who spun

145

rainclouds on her loom. His Uncle Witch-Witch had taught him this. Where was Witch-Witch? What was that muffled cry? His uncle had wanted to live, but he couldn't let him. He must keep choking Witch-Witch until all his breath was gone. . . .

The rain dance. It was so foolish, really. If the rain was coming, it would come. If it wasn't, no amount of conjuring would bring it. And to think he'd spent a lifetime convincing the tribe that he had power! Power was a hard thing to hold in one's hand. He clenched his fist. Hard to hold or not, he must use the power they *thought* he had until his last breath. *Power* . . . Ha! He couldn't even hold his own spirit on earth! It seemed to be floating away now.

A deadly fear gripped him. Would he ever live to see another rain? Giant fingers seemed to strike out in the night, suffocating him. . . .

The dim flicker inside the old doctor's tent provided little light, and the chieftain, making hurried preparations for the midnight dance, failed to see Peregrine Abelard's shadow slide by. He heard only the pop of a twig and supposed it to be a small rodent scavenging for food to assuage its hunger. Oh, for rain!

The chieftain checked his list to make sure everything was in order. The gods must be awakened. And how he hoped they would wake up in a good mood. He would certainly do his part to see that they did; he would follow the witch doctor's orders explicitly.

The low, sinister beat of the tom-toms began. Long into the night the sound would vibrate. It carried far: far enough, hoped the chieftain, to rouse those slumbering gods. The tribe *must* have rain at any cost. And soon!

The sound of the drums disturbed Lithia. She tossed and turned on her elkskin cot, her eyes staring into the gloom, her ears painfully alert. How could she sleep when nightmares of angry flames reaching out for her son scorched her mind? If only the white fugitive could have stayed with them! She had felt some strange passage of strength from him to her, and now that he was gone, she felt abandoned. A storm of confusion beat against her exhausted body and her feverish brain. She was torn between rage, self-pity, and despair.

The night was eerily still. Then a bloodcurdling yell split the unmoving air, and Lithia, caught between sleeping and waking, bolted upright and leaped from her bed. From the door of her pueblo she could see four tribesmen dancing with high steps in the light of a campfire. When someone threw a handful of dry sticks on the fire, the flame blazed up and showed their faces in sudden clarity. They waved tomahawks, wagging their heads and jerking their bodies with stiff gestures. They called to their fellow braves four by four: "Pah . . . pah . . . pah . . . pah . . ." There were sixteen in all, stamping the same savage steps, shouting the same wild yells. They trotted faster and faster around the bonfire, shot arrows at the moon and twisted their bodies until their heavy chests gleamed with sweat.

Broken Bow stirred, and Lithia reached out to still him, but when the noise arose to a chilling crescendo, he awoke shivering. "W-what is it, Mama?"

She held him to her but did not answer. *He's too young to understand; too old to be unaware. What shall I tell him?* Even the comfort of her arms could not stop his shaking; he pulled a blanket over his ears.

"Did . . . did they get the white man?" he mumbled from under the cover.

"No, I think it is just a rain dance. Keeta said there would be one tonight. Try to go back to sleep." *What did the white man say about the loving God? That He could help? That He would help?*

147

Measured by their fears, the night seemed a thousand hours long. Lithia pulled her cot close to Broken Bow and drowsed in fitful snatches, trying to shut out the evil sound outside.

When at last day dawned and Lithia, trying to brew some broth for herself and her son, heard the speeding hooves of the chieftain's horse, the beating of her heart seemed to stop. Some sixth sense told her that he had come for Broken Bow.

The sun, still a golden ball, scarcely touched the bottom limb of the eastern pine tree. Broken Bow turned his face to the wall, his stomach heaving. "Oh, God of the white man, if You are real, help me now!" he prayed frantically.

It was the dawn of a day the Kotopaxi tribe would never forget.

Chapter Twenty-Three

A Second Lie

The chieftain dismounted his steed and strode with cold disdain toward Lithia who had stepped outside her pueblo to meet him. He was taller than Victor had been, with wide shoulders tapering to a narrow waist. His height, however, seemed more than physical today. It accentuated his pride, his willfulness—and the sight of him could make anybody quake.

"I have come to settle the account with Broken Bow." His voice was as dry as the weather. Every fiber of him bristled while his eyes became pits of black fury. "Bring him out for me to examine. We shall see if your story *holds* water—or is *withholding* water!"

"But—"

"The gods are angry. The witch doctor is angry. *I* am angry. We are in the worst drought our world has ever known. No rain will come until the curse is removed from our tribe. We shall all die of hunger and thirst! Today is the twelfth year, the day the gods promised you in the vision that they would give your son a hand: a magic hand with great mystical powers. And if you have lied to me . . ." Even with his eyes squinted with the unfinished threat, Lithia regretted that the chieftain hadn't the decency to be bad-looking. It would make it easier if she had never felt a stirring in her heart for him.

She thought fast, her mind turning somersaults. Should she stall for time or make her confession and end the terrible waiting? She hadn't expected such an early encounter.

She couldn't hope to win a second gamble, but wouldn't it be worth a try? She had nothing to lose but her life anyway. So putting on an unflinching front as she had done six years earlier, she faced him.

"But not until the sun hangs in the top of the *western* pine tree, mighty chief. The gods are very *exacting*. That is when they will come *and not a minute before*. That is the time of my child's birth." Her palms seeped sweat.

It was a desperate bid for time, a random shot for a few more hours for herself and Broken Bow. No one knew the exact time of her son's birth except Mamu, and she was dead. The chieftain would have no way of knowing that Broken Bow was, indeed, born in the early morning hours when the sun was casting its first stippled rays over the forest; he had been away on a hunt when Broken Bow gave his first weak cry.

But wait! Was it possible that Keeta knew the time of the birthing? She had an unflappable memory, and she kept close tabs on Mamu. But since Keeta didn't know about the lie, she would have no occasion to give out the information.

The chieftain seemed momentarily disoriented. Someone had displeased the gods, and the sooner the tribe was rid of the hypocrite, the better. Then the rains would come. He was convinced (well, almost) that this beautiful, black-eyed squaw who still had the ability to make his pulse race was that someone. And his sufferance was wearing threadbare.

But, after all, he had waited six years. How could another few hours matter? The creek would not run dry before evening, and there was still enough food, although not in abundance, for the next few days. The gods had kept him from killing the boy once, and he must not take the remotest chance of angering them on the day that they (how he doubted it!) were to do him the greatest of favors. That battle that was to bring about his death—he saw no evidence of it.

He looked deep into Lithia's eyes, searching for deception, but she had hidden it so well that he was not able to find it. Even the dreadful fear in her heart was completely concealed. "Before this day is spent, we will *know.*" Like a knife, his words slashed without mercy.

The chieftain mounted his horse and rode away, choking on dust-laden air. He peered into the cloudless sky then let his gaze fall to the charred ground that gaped with cracks. When the tribe was at last purged of the curse, all would be normal again. Gods were easily offended, so fractious that one tired of their whims! Oh, well, before the sun set, they would be pacified.

They'd better get busy putting a hand on that piddling boy if they intended to do so, or else there would be a great bonfire when the sun went down. The chieftain suffered a pang of regret that he'd have to kill the squaw, too. She clung to his heartstrings. Yet she would never be content in his pueblo after he had killed her child. And as a timely lesson to other squaws, he must punish her for defrauding him.

If Lithia had made a goose of him before his tribe, it would be a good lesson for *him,* too. Never again would he listen to the tale of a simpering mother trying to protect her offspring.

151

If Lithia had *dared* lie to the hierarchy of the tribe, profaning the wise gods . . . The more the chieftain thought of it, the more infuriated he became. No, that squaw would never live to tell another lie regardless of her fetching manners and beautiful face. Her heresy would have no followers from henceforth and forever.

Lithia had, indeed, told a second lie to the mighty Kotopaxi chief. The first lie stretched over a few short years, the second over a few long hours.

Time was running out.

Chapter Twenty-Four

Keeta's Visit

As the hulk of horse and rider subsided in the distance, Lithia's face mirrored her mind: a commingling of anger and helplessness. Entering the pueblo, she dropped to her knees beside Broken Bow, who retched with fright. She put her arms about him, and they huddled together, the breakfast cold and forgotten. They were nomads in a wilderness of dread.

"Let's pray to the white man's God," Lithia said. "We have nothing to lose; our gods are powerless. They cannot hear us."

"But how can we approach the white man's God when we have no love, only hate and lies?" Broken Bow's thin fabric of thought was ripped with pitiful despondency.

"We will go to God in honesty and purity of soul. We will ask Him to forgive us for our hate and help us forgive others, too," Lithia said simply. "The white man said he would ask his God to protect us. Perhaps he is petitioning his God on our behalf right now."

"But will we not anger our own gods if we seek help from another?" The boy yearned to please the proper authority; his life depended on it.

"How can we anger gods that are no gods at all? They don't even exist. We could do better to pray to *each other* than to a piece of wood. At least, we are living beings!" Hers were acid-soaked words. "Away with them!" She picked up a small carving and flung it into the oven.

What blasphemous words she spoke! Yet the heedless idols had not helped her when she needed them the most. She would worship them no longer. They were lifeless, a hoax invented by the witch doctor, and a waste of time. She had served false gods, a figment of someone's imagination, quite long enough. Away with them forever!

Together Lithia and Broken Bow prayed aloud to the white man's God. Humbly, childlike, they asked for a change of heart, for a love to replace their hate and to be worthy of a God so gracious. Lithia made a candid apology for her lies. "I will never tell another lie, loving God," she promised, "Even if it means death for me and my son." Her repentance was genuine.

An overflowing peace swept through the pueblo and caught both of them in its gentle current. "I am not so afraid now." Broken Bow lifted awe-filled eyes when they had finished the prayer. "I have trust in our new God. I feel His love for a poor broken bow."

"Yes," Lithia agreed. "I have never felt so clean—like a washing *inside* of me. The hate is gone."

Still reveling in her newfound righteousness, Lithia didn't hear the thud of moccasins or see Keeta slip through the door. She was unaware of her presence until she spoke. "To whom were you speaking so loudly, Lithia?" she asked.

"I was praying, Keeta." Lithia lifted her head high; her

eyes shone with a warm light that radiated through her.

"To which of the gods on the totem pole were you appealing?"

"To none of them, Keeta. And to none of the trees or stones or insects. I was talking to the true God who is made only of love. There is only one God, and He lives in the heavenlies. All other gods are no gods at all. The totem is powerless; it is no more than a piece of wood that can be burned in the fire or chopped with a blade."

Keeta's mouth dropped open. "Who would dare?"

"I would. I cast my worthless idol into the oven today."

"Are you *denying* the tribal gods, Lithia?"

"I think it would be impossible to deny a *nothing.*"

"It is blasphemy! How could you think of doing such an atrocious thing? It is the worst of all transgressions."

"If they *were* gods, that would be true, of course."

"Are you telling me that you are spurning *our gods?*"

"I have given my heart to the God of love."

Keeta's eyes hardened. "And I noticed that the chieftain came to visit with you this morning while the tribe slept. He is a married man, Lithia. If I should report this to his wife, Essence, she would make trouble for you. And I wouldn't blame her. Anyone who lures another's husband away—"

"That is not so, Keeta. The chieftain came for quite another purpose."

"I know that you have some secret agreement with the chieftain. It is whispered throughout the camp. Otherwise, why would he let *your* child live when he wrenched my poor blind baby from my arms as I begged and screamed—and fed his body to the flames? My baby was no more cursed than yours!" She jabbed a finger at Broken Bow.

It was as if Keeta's foray fell on deaf ears. The placid

smile never left Lithia's lips; she seemed in a trancelike euphoria. Had she boiled the wrong weed and drank of its potent liquid?

"A brok—" Suddenly Keeta stopped short, leaving the word dangling as she espied the wooden hand of Broken Bow. So! All these years, Lithia had presumed to trick the chieftain. Unless one stood very closely and was very observant, the hand would pass for a real one.

This farce must be reported to the chieftain at once. It wasn't rumor: she had learned for herself that Lithia was trying to fool the chief. It was her duty as a loyal squaw of the Kotopaxi tribe to report such mischief. Besides, if her own blind papoose was put to death because of a birth defect, equality demanded that Lithia's son face the same fate. Right and fairness should prevail in any society. Broken Bow *should* have been destroyed years ago; Lithia had kept her son a dozen years too long already.

Death would not be an undeserving penalty for Lithia herself. She would certainly be put away with her son. Unless . . . unless . . . why hadn't she thought of that? As the chieftain's mistress all these years, Broken Bow might be the chief's own son. Ah, now it was all coming together. . . .

Keeta, already nettled because the initiation of her adored son had been postponed, was ready to ignite trouble and let the ashes fall where they might. At best, she could tattle to the chieftain about Lithia's sacrilege. *That* would be a strike against her. She had openly admitted to turning her heels on the sacred pole. *That* should be enough to send her to her execution. The chief couldn't scuff dust in the face of decorum. Once reported to him, some disposition would have to be made of Lithia.

Keeta cut her visit short, reasoning that she wouldn't want to be caught sympathizing with a reprobate. In truth, she was anxious to find the chieftain and share her discovery with him. *Then* let Lithia smile like a simple-ton.

She said her goodbyes tersely, but Lithia, becoming more and more filled with God's love, never suspected the evil intent of the tribe's gossipmonger. Even if she had, it could not have shaken her trusting heart now.

Chapter Twenty-Five

Keeta's Report

Keeta's discovery, embellished to her own liking, went straight to the chieftain's ears. He was riding restively about when she hailed him to a halt.

"As a dutiful squaw in this superior tribe, O mighty chieftain, I need to have a conference with you," she began.

"Except it be of utmost importance, I have no patience for babbling squaws today," he snapped. He had never been overly fond of Keeta. "My mind stampedes with weighty matters."

"It is of *utmost* importance, sir."

"You understand that there has been no rain, that the gods are furious, and that anything less is trivial?" he bellowed. "I haven't time for female pettiness. If it is some ridiculous argument between you and your counterparts, be gone! I am trying to find answers!"

Fate had fallen to Keeta's side. "Oh, yes, great one, I understand. Perhaps what I have to report will shed some light on the problem. One can hardly blame our jealous gods for withholding rain when such irreverence runs rampant within our very ranks."

"What are you trying to say, woman? I dislike parables."

"Hear me out, mighty one. I just happened to be passing the pueblo of Lithia and her son today—"

"I was there at dawn. You can't tell me anything I don't know. The showdown shall come at sundown. Six years ago Lithia told me that the gods had come to her in a vision and promised a magic hand for her son on his twelfth birthday. That is today—"

The wooden hand. Ah, Lithia planned to fool the chieftain. What a sly trick! "But chieftain—"

"I am speaking. No squaw interrupts." His words curdled the air.

Keeta bowed low in apology.

"The papoose, she tells me, was born at the going down of the sun. I am waiting."

"Lithia's broken bow was born in the early morning hours, my honorable chieftain. When I saw the midwife, Mamu, hurrying to Lithia's place, I followed along to see if I might be of help. I was standing outside the door when the cry of Lithia's newborn, no louder than a kitten's mew, reached my ears. I could not stay; my own son needed my attention. But as I ran home, I looked toward the sky, and there hung the sun on the first branch of the *eastern* pine tree. 'It is good luck,' I said, 'because it is a morning baby.' If the gods were granting a magic hand, it certainly should have been given on time, wouldn't you think?"

The chieftain's face grew livid. "I shall go at once to arrest her! Look! The sun leans overhead to the west already. It is past noon."

"Please observe closely when you go, mighty chief.

That wicked woman planned to deceive you in the name of the gods. She has carved out a wooden hand that looks startlingly like a real hand. The magic is in her carving. Yesterday at evening's close, I went to her house, and she refused me entrance because she was working on the fraudulent thing. Hidden under a blanket was the stump of a tree from which she was sculpting the hand. She admitted that the knife was there with the wood." She paused to get her breath, intoxicated with the chief's attention. "And that's not the half of it."

"There is more?"

"Much more."

"I wonder that we ever had rain. You must tell me all."

"In the gray of night, I saw a man stealing from her dwelling. He sped like an arrow, and I couldn't see clearly, but I think he was a white enemy. His clothing was . . . different, and he wore no moccasins but rather a strange shoe. Lithia is doubtless plotting the overthrow of our tribe."

"Before the gods, you are telling me the truth?"

"I am, mighty one."

"That is all?"

"No. There is a sin worse than all I have mentioned."

"Worse? There can't be—"

"Yes. Lithia boldly denies every god on the totem pole. She says they are wooden nothings. Today I caught her praying—and quite loudly—to a God unknown to our tribe. She said the totem pole gods are *worthless* and *powerless*. Those were her exact words. Can you wonder that the gods are inconsolable? They have been insulted."

The chieftain thanked her for her information, something he seldom did. "I shall see that you are rewarded for your courage in reporting this to me," he said. "We shall honor your worthy son on the entrance of his manhood soon. I may even give him a new name and a special place in the tribe."

No words could have made Keeta happier. Triumph played in her face. "And if you would like to claim him as your own, O mighty chieftain—"

"My thoughts drift that direction."

The chief slapped his horse and left in a spiral of dust, his greed for action building. He ordered his sixteen dancing braves to gather wood for the burning ceremony of Broken Bow, which would be followed by a separate cremation for his dark-eyed mother.

"We will make sure that Lithia witnesses the death of her son before she is turned to cinders," he said, his eyes as cold as pebbles. "Then we will scatter the soot before the gods as a peace offering. I shall go for her now, and we will bind her with ropes and let her roast in the sun while we feast."

It had taken an extra effort to harden his heart against the squaw he had once envisioned his own, but he could not show weakness if he expected his tribesmen to show strength. Lithia had prescribed her own medicine, and she would get it.

He saw Slate walking toward him and reined in. "Come," he beckoned. "I commission you to go to every pueblo in the village and summon every member of my tribe to the powwow grounds for a celebration. Tell them to bring much food and a heart for festivity."

How dare a squaw lie to the tribal chief! His face became suffused and the veins on his temples swelled, distorting his good looks.

He gave his horse an angry kick. The animal reared and ran fast, but the speed was too slow for his master's seething impatience. *I'll show that traitorous woman who is boss around here!*

Chapter Twenty-Six

Danger!

Four hours of the twelve lay ahead for Lithia and Broken Bow. Neither expected the return of the chieftain until late afternoon. Lithia prepared a meal of ground acorn cakes and dried cow peas.

"Shall we try to escape into the woods, Mama?" Broken Bow asked.

"No," she answered. "We would surely be followed and captured. We will persevere to the end and trust our new God to give strength for whatever our punishment. If we die, we will die with Him in our hearts—and honorably," she said. There was another dimension to life, and of their tribe, only they knew its secret. "Sharing death with each other—and trusting God—will make it a great deal easier. Your father faced death bravely, and so shall we."

"Your courage cheers me, Mama."

"It will be good to have the uncertainty finished, my son. We will die, and that is a peculiar realization but at

163

the same time liberating. Nothing shall harm us beyond. We are now eating our last meal; we have seen our last sunset. It will soon be over."

"Yes, Mama."

Broken Bow, still overshadowed by the joyful release after their prayer, stepped out into the blistering afternoon sunshine, leaving Lithia inside.

In the dust-diminished distance, two hundred pounds of malice rode expeditiously toward their pueblo. Broken Bow stopped in his tracks. What could the chieftain's mission be at this time of day? It was yet four hours until . . .

The chieftain's eyes flashed with fire when he got close enough to see for himself that the talebearing squaw's report was true. Here, before his very eyes, stood the pallid boy with a pretentious hand made of wood!

It *did* look like an authentic hand. From a distance one could be easily misled. Even *he* might have been tricked if he had not known the truth of the matter. Lithia could have made a name for herself carving gods. But thanks to a trusty squaw's close scrutiny, the parody had been detected in time to save further curses—and to save his own face.

Lithia had set out to make him a laughingstock before the whole tribe. No man liked to be mocked. The woman would get her comeuppance. He would have the last laugh while she fried.

Where had she found the daring to delude a chief? As if a lie, followed by a second lie, was not enough. Ah, but she had *lived* a lie for twelve long years. The gods had been longsuffering. Little wonder there had been no rain . . . and that the rivers were drying up to puddles of gray mud . . . and that the animals deserted the country in search of food. Surprising there had been rain for the twelve cursed years. The gods were certainly more lenient than he would have been.

The chief would reaffirm his supreme tribal position this day. The boldest squaw would know there would be no exceptions for "visions" in the future, gods or no gods. From henceforth, if the gods wished to impart a message, they could come to him by personal appearance or with an audible voice. No mortal would again sidestep his cardinal rules.

Essence must not know of his plans for tonight. She would whine and wheedle if she did. He couldn't abide her tears. She had a heart of mush for children. She didn't understand the Kotopaxi policies and grieved the loss of any life for whatever reason. Essence was dear to him, but she was wrong. . . .

As the chieftain neared, Broken Bow's eyes were riveted to the firesticks hanging from the chieftain's waistband. These would start the death fire. He hoped that his mother would not have to suffer long.

Lithia, baking the cakes inside the pueblo, heard the clatter of the mustang's hooves and knew that something was amiss. At the threshold, her feet stuck to the earthen floor. Smothering a gasp, she forced herself to the door, pushing back the blackness that coiled around her. *The chieftain* . . . with fatal readiness. His hesitations were past.

In a fit of unbridled temper, the chief bounded from his horse and strode with mad determination toward Broken Bow. His hands knotted into fists, and he gritted his teeth.

The sickening hiss of a rattlesnake caught Broken Bow's attention. The viper was coiled to strike, his head high, his tongue flicking. Hearing the solid whir and sensing danger, the horse whinnied and pawed at the ground.

Broken Bow had never seen a snake so large; it was as thick as the chieftain's arm. Its dark, checkered body, rusty brown and black, was outlined with yellowish scales. Though it rattled its omen vigorously, the chieftain did not see the serpent. In his blind fury, he walked directly into its path.

Broken Bow didn't hesitate. He knew what he must do. Swifter than the evil rattler itself, he flung his own body between the deadly viper and the chief just as the snake struck. The chief saw the beast as it hit Broken Bow and knew what had happened.

The poison-filled fangs sank deep into the wooden hand, knocking the boy to the ground with a hard impact. Broken Bow scrambled up again. Acting impulsively, he seized a stone with his left hand. Hitting and hammering with all his might, he dazed the snake with blows on its writhing head. "Oh, God of love, help me save my chief!" he cried aloud. In the doorway, Lithia sobbed out an entreaty. She could see Broken Bow's heart pulsating in a little hollow of skin below his breastbone.

Only temporarily maimed, the snake tried to recoil and repeat the strike in a fight to the finish. The air trembled with the hissing sound; the stallion snorted and backed away. Then, recovering from shock, the chief killed the snake with his tomahawk.

The snake lay dead; it measured as long as the chief was tall. The fangs would be bragging booty for the waistband of the most fearless brave. The bevy of rattlers would be a prize for the witch doctor himself; a rattle so magnificent would drive away the most obstinate of illnesses. And a mere boy had tackled it singlehandedly.

Lithia's feet still clung to the floor of her pueblo, refusing to become untracked. She was unaware of the hot oven smell of her cakes turning to brown, oblivious to the parched cow peas. Her son had done a noble deed; he had saved the chief's life, and she was proud of him. His strength—and his nobility—came from the loving God.

The chieftain turned from the snake to Broken Bow. "Why did you not let the snake kill me when you knew that I had come to kill you?" he asked, shaken from his close brush with eternity. "Had I died, Essence would have said that you were meant to live and she would not have allowed anyone to harm you."

"Except for the Jesus God, I probably would have," admitted Broken Bow. "But He asked us to love our enemies. I prayed to the loving God, and He gave my heart forgiveness. And now I love you and would not want to see harm come to *you* even though I am doomed to die myself."

"The loving God? Is that the God who made your wooden hand?" the chieftain asked, now ready to accept any explanation for the hand that stood between him and sure death.

"No, a white man who escaped your poisoned arrow yesterday in the woods gave me the hand," the boy said. He and Lithia had promised God they would tell the truth. "He was a Christian missionary. See the mark left by your arrow?" Broken Bow held out the hand, and the chieftain bent low to examine it.

The sight made Lithia's heart turn over with an odd thump. The great man and the slight boy with their heads together made a picture she had often dreamed of. She closed her eyes against an unnamed pain.

"Yes, it was my arrow that made the cut," the chieftain said. "I'm glad I didn't kill the missionary."

"Oh, God wouldn't let you!" said Broken Bow. "It was the missionary who told Mama and me about a good God—all made of love—who takes care of broken bows

167

like me. We prayed to Him, and He filled our hearts with a most marvelous peace. And now we are not afraid to die."

"*I* was . . . afraid when I met death just now."

"It is because you don't know *our* God. He isn't at all like the totem gods who are no gods at all."

"I'd like to know Him." The chieftain looked up to see Lithia stuck in the doorway, her mouth a little open, her dark eyes wide with surprise. His eyes met hers: met and were drawn into their transcendent depths. The world was locked out.

When she still did not move, he smiled and motioned for her to join her son and him beside the enormous snake, battered from the blows of the tomahawk. Then, troubled by her tear-stained face, he said gently, "Do not fear, Lithia." Kindness framed his words. "This day has changed my life.

"I have been a foolhardy chief, and I am responsible for much needless grief. Essence tried to tell me I was wrong, but I would not listen. Your son shall live, and there shall be no needless killings in the future. I beg your forgiveness."

Only one who had lost and regained could know the sort of thrill that Lithia felt at that moment. She dropped her eyes lest the chief see her heart in them. If only he had abandoned his senseless rule sooner . . . before his marriage to Essence.

"I don't deserve your forgiveness," he said. "And I will understand if you cannot—"

His humility enchanted her, disordered her heart, intruding a fear there lest her control should break. "You are forgiven." She said it softly.

"We will have a great feast of celebration for the young brave who has saved my life this day," he continued. "The wood is ready to roast the venison. I must go to ignite the fire; the tribesmen are waiting."

He lifted his nose into the air and sniffed. "I smell rain. We must hurry with our feasting, for the rain is but a few hours away."

Lithia's heart missed a beat in its rejoicing.

The chief moved closer to her until they were face to face. It was the most natural of all things for him to lean over and give her a kiss. Her whole being seemed to burst into flame.

Chapter Twenty-Seven

The Victor

"Your son will ride with me, Lithia." The chieftain lifted Broken Bow onto the horse and smiled again—a smile so tender that Lithia could not swallow. "I will give him the best of care."

No one save the chieftain had ever sat astraddle the mustang's back, but the animal accepted Broken Bow as if he had a right to be there. Indeed, it seemed he bore his burden with prancing pride.

The ground below seemed so far away that Broken Bow might have been frightened except for the powerful arms that encircled him. Is this the way a father's arms would feel? His heart seemed to swell and push against his ribs at the risk of bursting. "Thank you, Jesus, God of love," he murmured as the wind stroked his face. He had never been happier.

The chieftain, a novice at showing affection, nonetheless hugged the boy close to his rock-hard body. His thoughts cranked out plans faster than he could sort them. This thin, frail child must be nourished to health. That would be his project.

On the outside, the boy was weak, it was true. Yet inside the boy, the chief sensed a love stronger than any power he had heretofore encountered. Anyone given muscle and sinew, could be strong on the *outside*. But it took a special bow to be strong *within*. Isn't this what Essence had been trying to tell him all along? She was right, for today the chieftain recognized that he was riding with a Bow much stronger than himself.

Seated in front of the chieftain, Broken Bow had waved a cheery farewell to his mother. Her cheeks glistened with tears, but they were happy tears. It seemed that her hollow black eyes were coming back from a long trip. It had been a hard twelve years for her. Years of pain. Years of worry. Years of heartache. But since he would be permitted to live, her son would make it up to her: he and the loving God.

The fire sticks bumped together in rhythm to the stallion's steady trot. It sounded to Broken Bow as if they were praising God, too.

Broken Bow had wanted his mother to come along with them, but she said she must get food gathered for the festivity.

Lithia cherished the private moments. She needed time to disarm the chieftain's kiss that shot through her like a bolt of lightning, striking her heart. She wanted to excuse it as a kiss of gratitude. The chief's senses were sharpened by the narrow escape, and he had acted impulsively. She must not hold him accountable for that single deed.

God had forgiven her of so much; it seemed she had shed a great load. She felt weightless enough to run through the forest and jump over the tallest tree. She was glad for this time alone to give thanks to Him.

Her lies were wrong, and she would make amends. She would show kindness to Keeta, too. Keeta didn't know the loving God, but Lithia longed to tell her about Him. Keeta would be a good one to help spread the news. Her love for tattling might come in handy.

When the chieftain left Lithia's pueblo, his heart did not leave her there. Thoughts of her beautiful face possessed him. "Do you think that you would like to be my son?" he asked Broken Bow.

The boy didn't answer at once, but the chief could feel him thinking it over. When he did reply, it was with conviction. "No, your honor. I must grow up and provide for my faithful little mother. She has no one but me, you see."

"Do you suppose that she would let *me* provide for her?"

"No, your honor. She would not wish to be a burden to you. We will make it, the two of us."

"But what if I should make your mother my squaw?"

"She would not be happy, your honor," the boy said, remembering that Keeta said the chieftain already had a wife.

"Why would she not be happy? Have I so crushed her spirit that she could not love me?"

"She could not love you because you already have a wife. Keeta said so."

Keeta. A woman who didn't always tell the truth. Yet she knew how to interlace her lies with truth. Or sometimes she would tell the truth as though it were a lie so that when she was caught, the truths covered for the untruths. . . . What had Keeta told about Essence?

The chieftain rode on in silence, a captive of his own thoughts, until they reached the midst of the village. The tribesmen were milling about restlessly, watching for the return of their chief. The wood for the burning of the victims was in order. The first spark must be kindled by the chief, an honor he reserved for himself alone.

Making her way from her pueblo to the ceremonial grounds, Keeta was feeling remorse for spilling the tell-tale news to the chief. What if she were in Lithia's moccasins today? Her pricking memory played back the fateful day fourteen summers ago when her own child was burned. Now she wished she'd disciplined her prodigal tongue. It would give her no pleasure to witness Lithia's death. She ventured a prayer in Lithia's behalf, a prayer to the totem pole gods that Lithia had shamelessly denounced.

The waiting tribesmen welcomed their leader as he approached, each bowing a salute. He had brought his victim to be burned. But where was the woman? And why was the chief's countenance changed? The fury was gone; his eyes were alight. They waited. . . .

Gathering them about, the chieftain told of Broken Bow's heroic deed. The tribal members responded with whoops of joy. "The spirit of his father dwells in him," they said. "Victor saved the chief from death, and now his son follows in his footsteps."

"We shall have the greatest celebration the Kotopaxi tribe has ever known," proclaimed the chief. "We have never had greater reason to rejoice as you shall see before the night falls upon us."

Lithia came, wearing her prettiest dress, a dress she had put away when Victor died. Seated with the chieftain and Essence, she and Broken Bow were served first. They were moments worth hoarding, and she thought that Broken Bow would never have a greater birthday than this. Special seeds and nuts, preserved only for high ceremonies, were brought, and although the food was scarce, the chieftain said there would soon be plenty more. Only the loving God could perform such a miracle!

Broken Bow accepted the honors given him with humility, knowing the praise was not his own. He had done nothing but fend off a snake. It was God who turned the chief's heart about. If only the white man could know about today's deliverance! Perhaps someday, by some means, he would learn that Broken Bow had been awarded the coveted headband of a young brave, a headband that sported an eagle feather.

Each brave in turn shook Broken Bow's left hand, casting envious glances at the carved right hand's distinguishing marks. The wooden hand had saved two men from death. Was it not of more value than a hand of flesh that could be easily damaged?

Keeta's son, Slate, sulked. He had lost the envied position of future chief. The chieftain would adopt the boy who saved his life. Nothing had turned out right for him; he'd lost his pole and his place. Grudgingly, he admitted to himself that the race went to one with a better heart than himself. *He* wouldn't have saved the life of a chief who planned to kill him. In fact, *he* wouldn't have saved the chieftain at any rate if he knew he would have his place in the tribe. Yet Broken Bow held no vengeance and sought no honors. How could this be?

In the midst of the feast, the chieftain received an urgent message. The old witch doctor had expired after his strenuous night of rain chanting. In his lifeless hand was the secret bundle, upon his face the evil-chasing mask.

At the news, the braves went into an excited dither. According to custom, a tribal council must be called at once to replace the doctor, for what a fearsome thing it was for any tribe to be unprotected from evil spirits even for a few hours! And who would replace the one they thought omnipotent?

The chief held up his hand for their attention. The

silence was like a sharp breath. "We will not need another witch doctor." His deep voice rolled across the vast throng. "The witch doctor shall be given the burial of a common tribesman tomorrow. Then we shall burn his tent and all the potions it contains. Each of you will bring your gods and cast them into the fire. We need no idol gods! We shall worship the faces on the totem pole no longer." His voice rose. "The son of Lithia, whom I will take as my own son, knows a God who will protect us even as He protected me this day. He is the only God we will ever need. Tell us of Him, Lithia!"

Lithia felt herself coming to life again; her strength crept back as the ravages of grief dripped away. In unadorned but powerful simplicity, she told all she could remember, gaining confidence as she went along. Words came to her mouth of their own as she told of the death of this One for all humanity, His resurrection—and His concern for earth's broken bows. He forgave. He didn't hold grudges or impose curses. He healed and loved.

The chieftain's adoring gaze never left Lithia, but she was so caught up in her ministry that she did not notice. Some of the squaws wept and the braves wiped their eyes, forgetting that emotion was forbidden. Even Keeta was glad. Never again would a mother's heart be plundered as her own had been. Braves could grow old without fear. Willow sighed; the husband she had recently married would not be destroyed if he became injured. It was too good to be true.

"We will find the white man who knows about this wonderful God," the chief said. "We crave more knowledge. Wherever the missionary is, we will find him and fetch him."

"The God of love will send him back to us," Broken Bow said. "God sent him over the ocean to tell our tribe about His love. There is a whole book of stories about our God."

"We shall welcome the missionary—and we shall welcome this God," the chief flung his arms wide. "The missionary will be our spiritual leader in place of the witch doctor. We will learn to be strong *inside.*"

A hush fell over the listeners as they hung on the words of their chief, rich in looks and authority and now with a splendor of spirit that they couldn't quite place but they could feel.

The sky danced with a first streak of lightning announcing the approach of rain. Excitement ran through the tribe. "The rain is coming! The rain is coming!"

"Listen, my people. Victor, the brave who saved my life, left behind a beautiful squaw who bore him this lovely son after his death. I shall make his family my own. Lithia shall become my squaw."

Lithia, feeling Keeta's accusing eyes upon her, drew back as if she'd touched a hot coal. *I cannot become the chieftain's squaw,* her mind rebelled. *The God of love would not be pleased that I should occupy the pueblo of a married man. That would make Essence unhappy.* Love and anguish intermingled.

The chieftain talked on, but she could not lift her head. It had been enough that a married man had kissed her and that she had let her emotions enjoy the kiss. What was he saying? "My sister, Essence, is tired of making my johnnycake and she says that my pueblo is too large for her. Essence will move into Lithia's smaller pueblo. That is her wish."

His *sister?* But Keeta said—

Now he was speaking directly to her. "Please lift your eyes to me, Lithia. I have never before had a squaw nor needed one. But I need you, beautiful lady, to help me learn about the new God. I pray that my love for Him may someday equal my love for you." She looked up, but the bright intensity of his eyes was too much for her. His huge, expanding tenderness burst all the limits of feeling. Her hands flew to her face as a tingling sensation ran from her head to her toes.

"You *will* marry me, won't you, Lithia? I think that I cannot live without you. Together we will devour life like an apple picked from a tree. But you must hurry and say yes before we are washed away with the coming rain!"

She could not think, but she knew what she felt: this was good, and right, and forever. . . . She laughed, the first bubbling, carefree laugh in twelve years. "Just so we are washed away together, my handsome chief!"

A clapping of acceptance ran through the tribe, climaxed by a great clap of thunder. "Lithia, my love, even the heavens clap," teased the chief. The heady perfume of rain swept in on a blast of cool air that carried off the staleness of the long hot day.

The first drops of rain fell on the chieftain's ruddy face. "My people!" he shouted above the approaching cloudburst. "Today I have a new wife, a new son, and a new God!"

The tribe erupted with clapping, cheering, shouting. "Someday my son will be your chief . . . for he is the *victor,* and that shall be his name."

With a glorious dismissal, he swung Lithia into his strong arms as the moisture shone and beaded its way down his cheeks, cheeks flushed with pleasure.

Lithia pressed her face gently against his shoulder. Dreams that she had dared not clothe in words had come true. The name she loathed, the name that had branded her child an outcast—Broken Bow—would never be spoken again.

Then the chieftain marched through the jubilant

crowd calling out to his son, "Come along, my little chief!"

About the Author

LAJOYCE MARTIN, a minister's wife, has written for Word Aflame Publications for over 20 years with more than 200 stories and 19 books in print. She is in much demand for speaking at seminars, banquets, and camps. Her writings have touched people young and old alike all over the world.

Other Books by LaJoyce Martin:

The Harris Family Saga:
To Love a Bent-Winged Angel
Love's Mended Wings
Love's Golden Wings
When Love Filled the Gap
To Love a Runaway
A Single Worry
Two Scars Against One

Pioneer Romance Series:
So Swift the Storm
So Long the Night

Pioneer Romance:
The Wooden Heart
Heart-Shaped Pieces
Light in the Evening Time

Western:
The Other Side of Jordan
To Even the Score

Path of Promise:
The Broken Bow
Ordered Steps

Children's Short Stories:
Batteries for My Flashlight

Nonfiction:
Mother Eve's Garden Club
Heroes, Sheroes, and a Few Zeroes

Order from:
Pentecostal Publishing House
8855 Dunn Road
Hazelwood, MO 63042-2299